# METROSEXUALS

## JOHN WIGHT

Solid Ground Press

Copyright © John Wight 2023

John Wight asserts his right under the Copyright, Designs and Patent Act (1988) to be identified as the author of this work.

for Rab

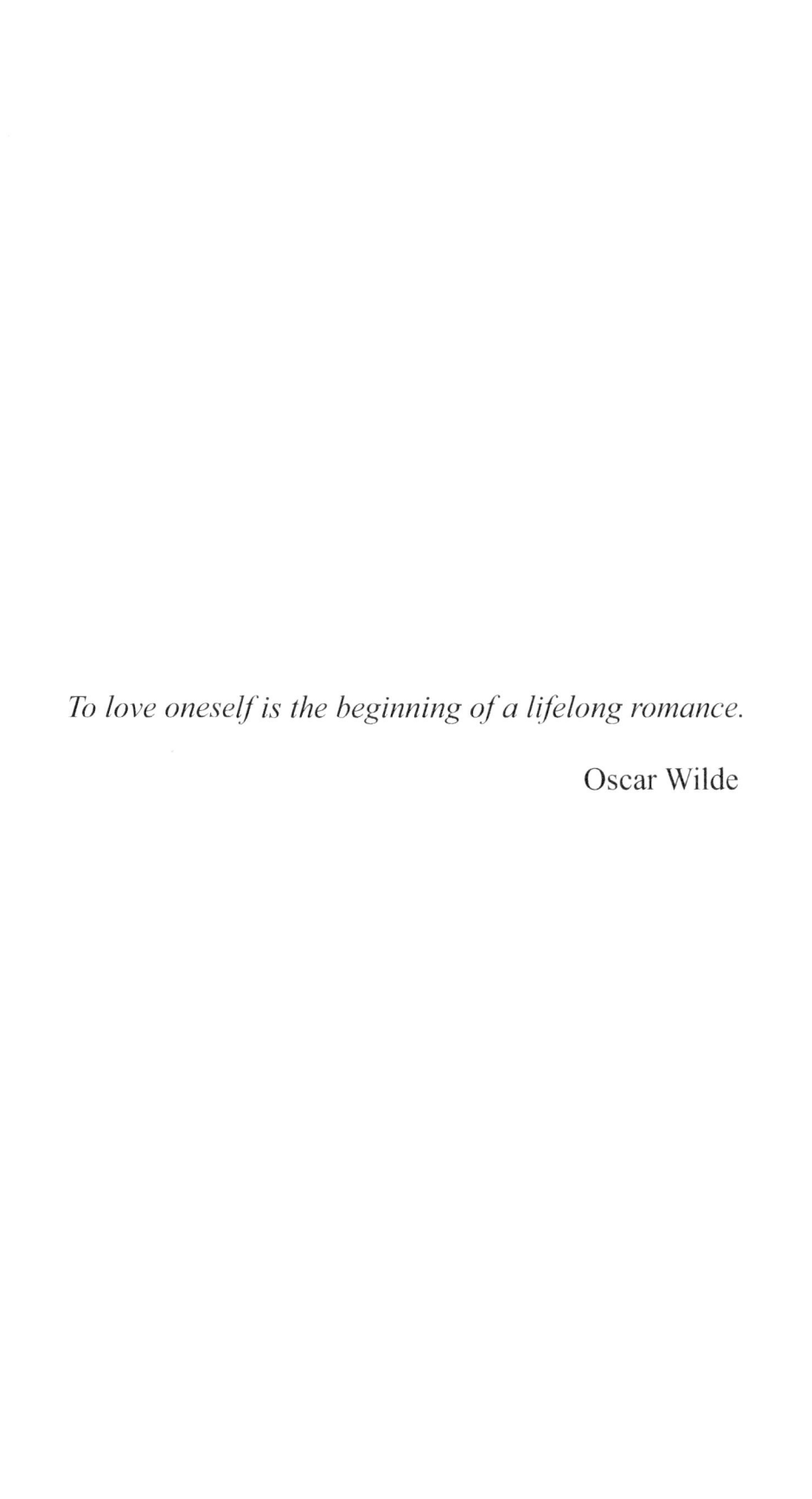

*To love oneself is the beginning of a lifelong romance.*

Oscar Wilde

# 1

*It is better to spend money like there's no tomorrow than to spend tonight like there's no money*

On the short drive into Edinburgh city centre on this Saturday night, Brian's mood was buoyant. His workout that morning had been excellent, completing his usual five miles running on the treadmill in 31 minutes and 23 seconds, shaving in the process four seconds off his previous personal best. His free weight workout after that had also been good; he'd felt strong and was able to handle more weight than normal.

Gareth suggested while they were relaxing in the sauna afterwards that his improvements were doubtless down to the new creatine powder he'd started taking on his advice. Brian agreed while ascribing his decision to introduce an extra rest day into his weekly exercise regime, thus allowing more time for recovery, as an additional factor.

Regardless of the cause the upshot was that he felt fitter, stronger and, most importantly, leaner these days. It's why that right now, on his way to meet the guys for another Saturday night out, he was buzzing.

## 2

Speaking of the guys, after their workout and sauna earlier, they'd enjoyed their regular Saturday lunch at Harvey Nichols. Pierre had reserved their usual table by the window with its panoramic view over the city. Sticking to his diet, Brian ordered salmon and stir fried vegetables, while Gareth and Gerry opted for their usual chicken caesar salad. As for Callum, he went a bit mad on the carbs in opting for the chef's special in the shape of a mushroom risotto. After lunch, washed down with some sparkling water and a glass of champagne each, they headed downstairs for some shopping.

Brian was the only one who didn't buy anything today, disappointed to come across a Paul Smith two-button light grey suit he liked only to find they didn't have one in his size. Gerry got himself a pair of Gucci jeans and a pair of Prada sunglasses, while Gareth picked up a new overcoat by Armani left over from the sale that was a snip at just under six hundred quid.

I'll make up for it next week, Brian thought as he turned his Audi into Charlotte Square, driving round to the north side, parking directly opposite Bute House, the official residence of Scotland's First Minister. The Georgian splendour of the building, of the entire block in which it was located, was lit up like an oasis of the Scottish Enlightenment that was asscociated with the city's New Town. As he parked, Brian pondered over whether Gareth would come across with his promise to wangle an invite for the boys to one of the official receptions held there on a regular basis, attended by the nation's business and political elite.

Just as he removed the key from the ignition, his phone beeped with an incoming text from Pamela.

> *hi babes. change of plans. out with the girls in edinburgh tonite. hope to see u in lulus later? P xx.*

Shit, she was supposed to be going to Manchester this weekend. I've arranged to hook up with Laura tonight.
Shit!

Brian sat in the car chewing over the dilemma that had just been landed on his lap. Laura he first met last month, when she was up from London for the weekend. She was sexy, tall with a nice figure. An executive with Louis Vuitton, she was originally from Edinburgh and came up every month or so to catch up with friends and family. She was good in bed, pretty fucking wild in fact, and certainly good enough for a rematch.

But Pam's hot, he pondered. On Thursday she turned up at the flat in a tight red halter top, white jeans and red heels. At five-ten with the body of an Amazon, my cock jumps straight to attention as soon as I look at her. The only downside where she's concerned is her propensity to let one go. Last time we were in bed she didn't even have the decency to get up and go to the bathroom. Just farted right beside me as if it was perfectly all right, blaming the laxatives she'd been taking to keep her weight down. Bad enough I've got to deal with people who fart and shit all over the place at work. There's no way I'm going to put up with it outside of work as well.

Brian was agitated and gone, suddenly, was his buoyant mood. Bloody women, he thought. Selfish. Every single one.

Fuck it, he thought finally as he got out of the car. I'm not going to let them spoil my night. Got a good mind to send them both on their way and see what else is out there.

The beginning of May, 2008, and it was a beautiful night in Scotland's capital. The city centre was packed with groups of men and women out on the town. Edinburgh was a popular destination for hen nights and stag nights, and normally they kept to the bars and clubs located in and around the Grassmarket. George Street — with its upscale bars, restaurants, clubs and boutique hotels, charging upscale prices — was the preserve of a more sophisticated crowd. It was a status protected by a much stricter door policy.

This is why, upon crossing the road from Charlotte Square and entering George Street, Brian was surprised and dismayed to see a hen night heading his way. There must have been around ten of them, loud drunk women staggering along the street with the bride-to-be dressed in some typically silly outfit. Distinct Geordie accents revealed Newcastle as their place of origin.

Putting his head down, Brian kept walking in an effort to pass as quickly as possible. Unfortunately for him, it didn't work. One of the hen party noticed him and made a beeline in his direction.

"Ayyup luv." she drunkenly declared. "Wanna cop a feel?"

Walking towards him, she lifted her top to reveal two massive mammaries, which she bounced around in front of his face. Brian edged around her and resumed walking. As he did, she helped him on his way with a grope of the arse, causing him to jump. He kept going, focused on getting away as quickly as possible with what was left of his dignity intact.

Brian Davison never imagined that he would be living like this at 36. Like most this age, he imagined himself married with kids and a nice house somehwere in the suburbs. He imagined two holidays a year, a car each for him and his wife, and his kids ensconced in one of Edinburgh's abundant private schools.

Funny thing is, most of the aforementioned he had already achieved. His kids *were* at a private school and they and their mother *did* live in a house in the suburbs — just not with him. He and his ex, Gail, had separated two years previously and he'd been happily single ever since.

Normality, he'd decided, had no place.

No, not for him Saturday nights in front of the telly with a beer in one hand and the remote in the other, sitting there waiting for your takeaway to arrive, if you're lucky getting your end away once a month with the same woman you've been having sex with for years, bored shitless but scared to admit it because of what your friends, family and people at work might think.

"Evening all."

Brian arrived outside Tigerlily to find Callum talking to Big Mark, the head doorman. The usual Saturday night queue of people waiting to get in was off to one side, while the pavement in front of the entrance was crowded with people who'd just left and were in the process of making up their minds where to head next, or others who were trying to blag their way in ahead of the queue.

"Mark says the place is packed with honeys tonight," Callum announced in response to Brian's arrival.

"Really?"

"Aw, the fanny's wall to wall tonight," Mark reassured him. "Wall to wall."

8

Big Mark was head doorman at Tigerlily, the place to be seen in George Street, and so it was always worth spending a few minutes chatting to him on the way in.

"How's the training going Mark?" Brian inquired. "You look like you've put on a bit of size."

"Aw, the training's going well pal — really well."

"Any fights coming up?"

"Aw, hopefully in a month or two, eh. Ah'm choking to get back in there — fuckin' choking."

"Make sure you let us know. We'll come along and support you. Isn't that right Callum?"

"Absolutely," Callum obliged. "Wouldn't miss it for anything."

"Aw, cheers guys. That would be brilliant."

"Well," Brian said to Callum, "what are we waiting for?"

"I'm not sure Gareth and Gerry are here yet. Mark hasn't seen them. I've tried calling, but they're not picking up."

Big Mark interceded: "Aye, but I was away grabbing a bite for half an hour, mind."

"Think we should wait?" Callum said.

Brian looked at him.

"Fair enough," Callum continued. "Mark, we'll talk to you later."

"Right guys, no worries. Have a good one, eh."

And with that they approached the steps leading up to the front door and walked in past the bouncers ahead of the queue, just as they did every Saturday night.

Inside the place, sitting at a reserved table way in the back with the place heaving around them, Gareth and Gerry were in the company of two girls they'd only just met. The two of them were engrossed in conversation, though more with each other than the girls.

"No-no you're wrong," Gareth was telling Gerry emphatically. "The best skincare products on the market are by Clinique. I use their face protector every day and swear by it."

"You're talking out your arse," came Gerry's retort. Clinique's products are overrated. I switched to Dermalogica months ago and the difference has been phenomenal."

At this point one of the girls, Emily, attempted to intervene. "Would you like to hear what we think?"

"No," Gareth and Gerry replied in unison.

"Look," Gerry went on, returning to the topic at hand, "Dermalogica use too much alcohol in their products. It irritates the skin, leaving it more susceptible to wrinkling. There was an article on it in GQ just last month."

"You must be drunk."

"I'm not drunk."

"Dermalogica," Gareth reiterated, "is easily the best skin care brand out there. Their testing is more thorough, extensive, and scientifically rigorous than any other brand, including Clinique."

"You're wrong."

"I'm not wrong. I…wait, come on, you're doing it again."

"What?"

"Substituting subjective supposition for objective fact when you know you're losing the argument."

"That's not true," Gerry said, averting his eyes to the guy at the bar dressed in the same navy Farhi jacket he had in his wardrobe at home. Though quickly deciding that the jacket looked better on him than it did on the guy at the bar, Gerry made a mental note to get rid of it when he cleared out his wardrobe next week. Can't take the chance of being in a bar or restaurant in the same item of clothing as somebody else, he thought. How fucking humiliating would that be?

It was now that Callum and Brian arrived at the table.

"So much for meeting up outside," Callum announced.

Brian's attention was straight on the girls, giving them with a quick up and down of the eyes.

"Aren't you going to introduce us?" he asked Gareth and Gerry.

Gareth opted to do the honours. "Girls," he announced, "these two handsome chaps go by names Brian and Callum. Brian leaned across the table with his hand out, in response to which the girls reciprocated and shook his hand.

"Very nice to meet you," he told them.

"Guys," Gareth went on," these two lovely ladies are… I'm sorry," he said, turning to the girls with a mischevious grin.

"I'm Jenny, she's Emily," Jenny said, growing irritated.

"Jenny and Emily," Gareth repeated enthusiastically. "I knew it was something exotic."

The girls glared at him in response.

"Well, ladies," Gerry announced, "I'm afraid you're going to have to vacate. Our friends have arrived."

"Yes, it's been nice but we're going to have to say cheerio," Gareth followed up chirpily..

The girls got up abruptly from the table.

"Come on Jenny," Emily said, "let's go and find some real men to talk to."

"Have fun," Brian called as they stomped off, heels clacking as they went.

"So," Callum said, returning his attention to the guys, "another Saturday night is upon us"

"We tried Oliver John's new place on Queen Street earlier," Gerry volunteered.

"How was it?" Brian inquired. "I've eaten at his place in London. The sea-bass was fantastic."

"Yes, the menu's not bad. Wine list could be better, though."

"Nonsense," Gerry interjected. "The wine list's excellent."

"No it's not."

"Their selection of French whites is first class. I should know."

"You know nothing. Their selection of French whites is decidedly average. You judge a wine's quality by the grape, not its alcohol content."

"All right-all right," Callum declared, deciding to intervene. "Truce. For God's sake guys, truce."

Between Gareth and Gerry a struggle for supremacy raged that was near Darwinian in scope. They competed over women, clothes, fitness, careers — everything.

Gareth Cairns was a member of the Scottish Parliament, an MSP, and viewed his position not as an opportunity to serve his constituents but rather to serve himself. Gerry Scott was a criminal defence lawyer and partner in his own firm. Among a section of the city's criminal fraternity he was known as Kamikaze Scott —this on the basis that if you had him representing you in court, you were going down.

It was now that Angie, one of the cocktail waitresses, appeared at the table. "More drinks, guys?"

"Hello Ange," Callum said putting his arm around her waist. "You're looking hot tonight. A bottle of Moet and four glasses please."

Angie smiled and retreated in the direction of the bar to get the champagne, Callum watching her while wishing she would finally relent and agree to go home with him. In a tight black dress, black tights and four-inch heels — and with a fit gym-trained body — he wasn't lying; Angie was indeed looking hot.

Callum Wilson plied his trade as a property developer and was worth more in assets than the rest of the guys put together. He also had three children to three different women, who each hated his guts and did everything they could to extract as much of his money as they could. His was a life lived in constant pursuit and constant retreat from women. It was a state of affairs he wouldn't change for the world.

Tigerlily was now busy and the boys spent the next few minutes casting their eyes around the place, looking to see who was looking at them. As ever, there was an abundance of attractive women in the place, and as ever it was time to start planting seeds in the form of eye contact and suggestive smiles.

"I need the bathroom," Gerry announced, getting up from the table. "Someone pour me a glass while I'm gone." Turning from the table, however, he was immediately confronted by the sight of James Traynor.

"Awright?" Traynor accosted him gruffly. "Ye hear aboot ma wee brother, aye?"

It took Gerry a few seconds to get over the shock of suddenly encountering one of the Edinburgh's most notorious thugs and criminals here in Tigerlily, rather than in his office or at court.

"Eh…hi James. Yes, I did hear about your brother. I sent David over to St Leonard's to see him last night. He's due in court on Monday, I believe."

"Aye, but make sure ye dinnae send that fanny intae court wi um like last time. Ah want tae get him off wi this, ken what ah mean?"

"David's a very competent lawyer. However if you'd prefer, I'll be happy to deal with your brother's case myself."

"Between you and me, he did stab the boy. It wis self-defence, but. Ye understand that, eh?"

"Yes James, I do understand."

James grabbed Gerry's hand and shook it vigorously. "Right pal, take it easy. I'm in wi a couplae gadgies jist oot the jail and they're oot their nuts. Ah'd better get back over before they rip the face offay sum cunt."

With that, James Traynor turned and disappeared into the mass of bodies standing three and four deep along the entire length of the bar. Gerry's stomach was churning. He was joined by the others, who'd all been watching and listening from the relative safety of the table.

"What on earth was he saying there?" Gareth immediately asked no one in particular.

"I haven't a clue," Brian quipped "I'm not a linguist."

"James Traynor is not a man to be crossed," Gerry said, still reeling from the exchange.

"I wonder what moisturiser he uses?" Gareth asked with a wry smile.

"That Lacoste sweater he's wearing," Callum said, "So chic."

"It's the tattoos on the hands that do it for me," Brian offered next.

Gerry failed to see the funny side. "Seriously," he announced, "we should speak to Mark. "Ask him how characters like Traynor are getting in here now."

With that, he headed off to the bathroom.

Five minutes after he did, Angie reappeared with a bottle of champagne, four glasses, and the obligatory ice bucket, all of which she proceeded to lay down on the table.

"Angie, that's what I call perfect timing," Callum said with a smile. "Stick it on our tab."

Ange made a start on opening the champagne.

"That's all right," Callum told her, "we can do that."

"Okay," Angie said, stopping and laying the bottle back down on the table with a smile. "Enjoy."

"Listen, before you go," Callum said. "If you fancy a drink after work, you know where I'll be."

"Yes, I do," she replied. "Downstairs with your hands all over some girl."

"Some *lucky* girl," Callum corrected her.

Angie laughed before heading off.

"They know you so well," Gareth quipped in Callum's ear. As he did, Brian set about opening the champagne. Moments later, after popping the cork, he filled everybody's glass. Gerry returned from the bathroom just in time to join them in a toast. "Gentlemen," Brian announced "to us."

"To us," everyone repeated, before clinking glasses and taking their first sip.

"Mmm…bit warm but not too shoddy," Gareth said.

Callum said, "Moet's not my favourite, but it'll do."

"I prefer Krug myself," Gerry said. "Sharper taste."

"No it doesn't," Gareth said.

"Yes it does."

"Oh for fuck sake," Brian said.

Half an hour later the boys had left the table and were standing in full view of the bar, eyes roving looking to establish eye contact with various females dotted around the place. It was a spacious bar, tastefully and expensively decorated in a baroque style in keeping with its status as one of Edinburgh's premier boutique hotels. Plush seats were complemented by intricate wall coverings and fittings in a series of themed areas throughout the bar and restaurant area. The smoking patio was located through a glass door, which meant that Tigerlily wasn't plagued with that all too common and vulgar affliction of people standing in the street outside the entrance, smoking. Subdued lighting cast a warm and intimate red hue over the place, helping to create an atmosphere conducive to hedonism.

Tigerlily attracted people from far and wide; its bar and restaurant tailored to suit an upscale clientele. However, being Edinburgh, a city with cosmopolitan aspirations but just a little too small to completely expunge the existence of its underclass, people like James Traynor were still able to get in as a result of the simple fact that the doormen were shit-scared of him.

"Over to your left," Gerry declared to the others. "The girls at the table. They're looking over."

The others looked over to the four girls who were seated at a table some ten feet away. "The blonde looks all right," Gareth affirmed. "Nice tits."

"Suspension looks a bit dodgy, if you ask me," Callum said, looking at her legs.

Brian spotted another likely target. "What about the redhead over there," he said. "She's with a guy, but I think she could be persuaded."

They all looked over to the tall redhead in a tight red dress standing with a big guy who had his back to them. Periodically, she kept glancing over his shoulder in their direction.

"Who's she looking at?" Gerry said.

"Me, obviously," Callum replied.

"Why," Brian said, "do you owe her money?"

"I *am* money."

As this exchange was taking place, Gareth's eyes fastened onto a voluptuous dark haired beauty, who was looking straight at him.

"Okay gentlemen," he announced to the others without taking his eyes off the girl, "it's about that time. Don't wait up." And with that he was off, making his way through the crowd in her direction.

"Look at him," Gerry said disapprovingly. "Off at the first opportunity."

"Gerry," Callum said reproachfully, "what's happening? This is the third week running that Gareth's pulled before you. Maybe you need a new haircut?"

"That's an outrageous thing to say. I'm the man."

"Eh, I don't think so mate," Callum said, winking at Brian.

"Not anymore. In fact, me and the boys are starting to think you've lost it.

"That's right," Brian agreed. "It's gone. You're yesterday's news my friend"

Gerry looked at each of them in turn, suddenly worried, their words seeping into his brain and playing havoc with his ego.

"Fuck you," he announced assertively, at which Brian and Callum burst out laughing.

"Yeah go on, laugh," Gerry went on. "Very funny."

"Your face," Callum said. "You should have seen it. You looked like you were about to burst out crying."

"I'm going to get another drink," Gerry said. "You two are winding me up."

Downstairs from Tigerlily was Lulu, providing the opportunity for a late drink for those in the mood to keep the night going after Tigerlily closed at one. Owned by the same owners as Tigerlily, Lulu was a club designed with intimacy in mind — lush couches and seats, low lighting, low ceiling, and a door policy that brought new meaning to the word discretion. It attracted a mixed crowd and was, as with Tigerlily upstairs, popular.

Tonight, at just after one, the place was heaving. Rather than wait at the bar to get served, which given the mass of people doing the same would only have ensured a long wait for a drink, Callum called one of the cocktail waitresses over and slipped her a hundred pound note to make sure she kept them supplied.

Now they were standing against the wall, each sipping champagne, surveying the action taking place around them. It was time to get busy trying to pull and with this in mind, Gerry had his eye on a brunette standing with her back to a pillar halfway along the bar. She was standing by herself — her friends were on the dancefloor — and she looked nothing if not fit in a pair of tight jeans and tight black satin top.

"Right," Gerry declared, "time to do some damage." And off he went, leaving Brian and Callum behind as he made his way over.

Watching him, Callum opined, "He's having a bad night."

"Yep," Brian replied, "a clear a case of wounded dog syndrome."

Wounded dog syndrome describes the condition whereby women were able to detect the whiff of hesitation and self-doubt in a guy. This occurs when said guy is low on confidence and gives off a vibe, a scent akin to that of a wounded dog. Most women can instantly detect it whenever they encountered it, and most found it a major turn-off.

Sure enough, just a few minutes after leaving them Gerry returned, having been unceremoniously repulsed.

"She's married," he offered up.

"No she's not," Callum replied.

"She showed me her ring."

"She showed you the door."

## 24

It was now that the redhead Brian had spotted upstairs earlier approached from behind and tapped him on the shoulder.

"Aren't you going to ask me to dance?"

The second the words left her mouth Brian was in lust, smiling as she took him by the hand and began leading him in the direction of the dancefloor.

Callum called after him. "Gym, Monday?"

"Usual time," Brian called back, just before he and the redhead were lost in the crowd.

The woman's name was Davina and the guy she'd been with upstairs was her ex. He'd taken her out to dinner in an attempt to patch things up, but halfway through the evening she decided that she was definitely no longer interested and they parted company after a couple of drinks. It hadn't been pleasant, but she was adamant it was over and that was that.

Emerging from Tigerlily, she'd spotted Brian heading down the stairs to Lulu with his friends and on impulse decided to do likewise, thus leaving her ex, Colin, to grab a cab home.

Two hours later, he and Brian were back at her flat just off the Meadows, hands and mouths all over each other on the couch. "Hold on a second," Brian said at a certain point, pulling away. "Bathroom calls." And off he went, exiting the living room and walking along the hall, looking for the bathroom in the dark.

"Last door on the right," Davina called out. Following her directions he found it, flicked on the light, entered and shut the door. It was big and tastefully decorated, fitted with elaborate old-style taps and a bidet next to the toilet. He turned on the cold tap in the sink, leaned over and splashed his face. Then he straightened up and studied his reflection in the long, rectangular mirror that ran the entire length of the wall.

It was time to pop a blue one.

With this objective in mind, he reached round to the back pocket of his Prada trousers, unbuttoned it and put his hand inside. "Ah shit!" he declared in a loud whisper, responding to the horrible sensation that met his hand. The viagra tablet in his pocket was crushed. It must have happened when he fell back on Davina's couch when things began to get hot between them. Fuck!

"Hurry baby," Davina called through. "I'm horny."

Brian looked in the mirror, cursed his luck, looked down at the remains of the pill in his hand, and then cursed it again.

## 2

*Society prepares the crime, the criminal commits it*

Monday morning and Edinburgh Sheriff Court was packed. Small bedraggled groups of men and women were gathered in huddles outside the gated entrance. Deference to the cool morning temperature was expressed in hunched shoulders and hands stuffed inside pockets. Coats, hats, scarves, gloves and umbrellas were a rarity when it came to this particular demographic, even in mid-winter.

Year round, no matter the occasion, the preferred mode of dress for these consisted of a tracksuit, occasionally jeans, training shoes, and baseball cap. A conglomeration of scars, scowls, yellow teeth, pale skin, and hungry faces completed the picture, marking them out as proud members of the city's underclass.

There they stood, stealing a quick smoke before heading inside to join that day's procession of unfortunates passing in front of an apathetic sheriff to hear their fate for in the main banal petty crimes motivated by poverty and alienation, mostly committed against each other. They were harsh and grim and hard to feel sympathy for, as they cowered behind an aggressive exterior in a futile effort to hang onto a shred of self-esteem.

Gerry Scott, criminal defence lawyer, approached the building along Chambers Street, walking at a brisk pace from his car in response to the cool breeze. Dangling from his right hand was a calf-skin leather briefcase, while held under his left he had a pile of case files pressed against his side. Another week was about to get underway and, as ever, he was fucking dreading it.

He walked through the gates of the court into the small courtyard that lay outside the building, head down as he went, passing between the small groups of people huddled together smoking. It was always at this point that his skin began to crawl with disgust, and as he headed for the entrance to the court he had to suppress a powerful urge to be sick. On he went regardless, through one of the two big revolving doors into the building, where a long line of people stood just inside waiting to pass through the metal detectors and the obligatory security check.

Gerry bypassed them and walked in via a staff entrance, flashing his ID to the security guard as he went.

Edinburgh Sheriff Court, located in the heart of Edinburgh's Old Town, was a large purpose built facility. It comprised 18 courtrooms on three floors, housed inside a building that had been designed to blend in with the historic architecture surrounding it. It had also been designed to enhance the functional requirements of a busy legal system. Natural light streamed in through a glass domed roof, while the walls, floors and fittings were light in colour —this in a failed attempt to create a pleasant environment for those passing through its doors.

It was an attempt that fell short due to the fact that it was a building in which despair and desperation reigned, and as Gerry made his way downstairs to begin the depressing task of dealing with his clients, he almost felt that he could reach out and scrape it off the very walls.

On he went regardless, putting himself in the same zone he alsways did at this juncture. Just grit the teeth and get through it, Gerry, he urged himself. Just grit the teeth.

"Yo…Kamikaze!"

Gerry was walking through the concourse downstairs when he heard James Traynor's voice ring out from somewhere behind. Accompanied by an extra powerful wave of dread rising from the pit of his stomach, he turned to see Traynor waving excitedly from across the other side of the concourse while coming towards him. Following close behind was a pasty-faced girl in a purple tracksuit with bleached blonde hair, jaw moving furiously as she masticated a piece of chewing gum in her mouth.

"Morning, James," Gerry said, smiling in an attempt to mask his discomfort.

"We're in Court Six," Traynor declared, studying Gerry through the bleary eyes of a man who'd been up the entire night imbibing cocaine and alcohol.

"Yes, I know."

"How's it lookin'? Think you'll be able tae get 'im off?"

"I'll do my best. It'll come down to the CCTV evidence."

"Aye but make sure ye fuckin dae yer best, eh. It's my wee brar we're talkin' aboot, no some fuckin' bam."

"Shut up ya radge," the girl interjected, scowling at Traynor. "Stop tellin' the man how tae dae ays job. He kens what ays daein. He doesnae need you tae tell um."

"Shut up ya wee slag."

"Naw, *you* shut up!"

The girl was the girlfriend of Traynor's younger brother, the very same who was due in court later that morning on a charge of attempted murder. While he was on remand she'd moved in with James, ostensibly so that he could help her look after his brother's two young children. Unbeknown to Traynor's brother, they were also sleeping together. Now, standing in the middle of a packed concourse, they were arguing back and forth, oblivious to the commotion they were causing or the attention they were attracting.

"Shut up ya wee slag or I'll kick yer fuckin' hole in!"

"Just try it ya cunt, ah'll cut yer cock off!"

"Aye?"

"Aye!!!"

By now a couple of security guards and two police officers were making their way over. As soon as they arrived on the scene, Gerry used the opportunity to slip away and head for the sanctuary of a vacant interview room off to the side. As soon as he entered and shut the door, the silence and solitude embraced him like a warm blanket. He slumped down in a chair, placed his files on the desk and stared at the wall opposite.

"I can't do this anymore. I just can't."

Gerry Scott had been practising law for ten years. The money was good, too good to turn his back on, but the price exacted in terms of his personal happiness was crippling him. He'd thought that taking over his own firm with his partner, Frank Gaffney, three years ago would allow him to spend more time out of court than in, but this isn't how things had panned out.

If anything, due to the pressures of generating business, Gerry was dealing with the same amount if not more cases than he'd been prior to branching out on his own. He was in the contradictory position of reaping the rewards of society's legal aid provision, designed to ensure that people without means could access legal representation, and despising the very people whom he represented under said provision. People like the younger brother of James

Traynor, for example. The kid was an out and out scumbag yet here was Gerry, currently engaged in the attempt to get him off with attempted murder, utilising knowledge and experience gained after years spent working his arse off to make something of himself.

Most of his other clients weren't much better. Every day a procession of lowlifes walked into his office seeking legal representation — thieves, fraudsters, junkies, sociopaths — people more in need of a bullet than criminal defence. Forced to sit and listen as they attempted, in their crude and vulgar way, to intimidate and pull the wool over his eyes made him wish he'd opted for a career in finance or banking like his father before him. But, no, he had to go and plough his own furrow, filled as he was with grandiose notions of rising to prominence in the legal profession and setting the bar by which others measured themselves.

But instead of working on High Court murder trials conducted under the glare of publicity, Gerry Scott had spent his career dealing with low level petty crime committed by the most despicable and repugnant elements of society. It was so bad that after work he usually couldn't wait to hit the gym and punish his body to the point of collapse. Today, however, he had six cases to deal with in court and a four o'clock meeting with another client back at the office before he could even think about the gym.

Pulling himself together, he sat up in the chair and took a long, deep breath "Come on Gerry, focus," he told himself. "Legal aid pays for your flat, your car, the clothes on your back and your social life. All you need to do is fill out the form, get a signature, and send it off. It's as easy and simple as that. Legal aid is your best friend and you should never forget it. Don't let the bastards grind you down."

And with that he got up, straightened his tie, opened the door, and walked back out to face the madding crowd. Almost as soon as he did he came face to face with another one of his clients.

"Awright, mate," the young man said, eyes hanging down to his chest with the methadone that was coursing his system. "What's happening wi my case n that?"

Roughly a mile east of Edinburgh Sheriff Court on Chambers Street stood the Scottish Parliament. It was located at the foot of the Canongate in the shadow of Holyrood Palace, the Queen's official residence in Scotland, with the spectacular backdrop of Arthur's Seat lying just beyond.

Devolved government in Scotland and Wales was established in 1998 with the intention of decentralising various government functions and responsibilities in order to satiate the aspirations of people in Scotland and Wales for more control over their own affairs. Regardless, any such control was funded by Westminster through the disbursement of an annual bloc grant, which in reality reduced both the Scottish Parliament and Welsh Assembly to toy-town status as far as the administration of government was concerned.

With regard to the Scottish Parliament specifically, the spiralling cost of the construction of the building in which it was housed, originally budgeted to cost the taxpayer around £50 million but costing in the end around £450 million, in addition to the hoo-ha over the actual design, had set the tone. The MSPs themselves, seventy men and women earning a basic salary in 2008 of fifty-five grand a year plus expenses, had proved to be, by and large, a ragtag bunch of second-raters with the debating, administrative and political skills of your average student.

Gareth Cairns was halfway through his first term as Labour MSP for the constituency of Edinburgh Central. He'd only joined the Labour Party six months before his selection as a candidate. His father had been a Labour MP for 20 years before retiring from politics. Four of those years were spent as a member of the shadow cabinet. And though he'd always been a staunch supporter of the trade union movement, by the time the new kids on the block staged their coup to take control of the party and shift its guiding principles to the right, changing the name from Labour to New Labour in the process, like many within the party Gareth's father, Tom Cairns, was ready to exchange principle for power.

Indeed, the Blair years for Cairns and others of his persuasion were proof-positive that in order to achieve power you had to combine market economics with low taxation and other incentives for the nation's entrepreneurs and 'wealth creators'.

As for his old beliefs in social and economic justice, meanwhile, he agreed with Blair and the rest of them that the class war was over, a thing of the past, and that the focus in this day and age should be on equality of opportunity rather than outcome. Socialism had failed, the world was now a global village underpinned by free market capitalism, and in order to thrive a nation and its people had to be willing and able to adapt to this new reality.

With this in mind, Tom Cairms had done his utmost to ensure that his son was provided with everything possible to enable him to succeed in life. Not for Gareth the comprehensive school education his father had. Oh no, his dad was determined that his son would attend the finest schools in the land, beginning with Fettes College in Edinburgh. If Fettes was good enough for Tony Blair, he rationalised, it was good enough for his own son.

That Gareth failed miserably during his time there was besides the point. Just being able to boast that he'd attended such a prestigious school would give him the leg up required to take his place among the upper echelons..

Upon leaving Fettes, Gareth went on to Edinburgh University. Despite not having the relevant qualifications he was admitted under the university's special dispensation scheme —this after his father pulled the requisite strings. However, while there Gareth spent more time drinking and partying than he did studying, to the point where he left without completing his degree.

His father came to the rescue once again; this time securing his son a position as a trainee broker with an investment bank in London. He did so by calling in a favour from a former parliamentary lobbyist who some years before had managed to persuade Tom Cairns to vote for a bill permitting a new motorway extension in the southeast. The individual concerned knew someone who knew someone and, bingo, Gareth began his working life on a salary of forty grand a year plus benefits in the City.

This was back in the late nineties when business was booming, when the City of London was supported in its status as the world's most vibrant money market by Blair government via the implementation of the kind of economic policies that would have had Dick Turpin smiling in his grave in appreciation.

Gareth embraced the good times and soon develor penchant for Rolex watches, Paul Smith suits, fine and clubs. Soon enough, he developed a pattern of coming into the office late and leaving early, until one day he found himself in his boss's office being reprimanded. A phone call to his father from one of the directors resulted in a severe talking to by his father, leaving Gareth in no doubt that if he fucked up again his old man wouldn't be around to bail him out.

Suitably chastened, for the next year he buckled down, working diligently and even starting a serious relationship with a woman he met at work. In time even his father was satisfied with his progress, relieved that finally his son's future looked assured. His fall from grace occurred over incompetence with regard to an important investment in Burma, a deal he'd been given the responsibility of on the bank's behalf. Incompetence was the reason for his dismissal to minimise any city. In truth it was corruption in the form of had accepted from a certain Far East bank them to transfer the funds involved in earmarked for the role of conduit and the Burmese government —

which due to the nature of that regime obviously meant that everything had to be done on the quiet — filed a complaint. An internal investigation was launched and Gareth Cairns' duplicity was uncovered.

Soon after losing his job, down the pan also went his relationship. Fiona was more worried about how the impact of his sacking might affect her own career than she was about him, and so out the door he went. Given that it was her place they'd been staying at, Gareth found himself in a not-so-good situation.

So where now what now?

Gareth had a few grand in the bank; enough of a stash, if he was clever, to invest. A phone conversation with his old school chum, Callum Wilson, led to him returning to Edinburgh to start a new career in property development.

Callum was one of the biggest developers in the city and by this point worth a couple of million in assets. Like him, Gareth wanted to get rich from the property boom in that had earned Edinburgh the status of the second most expensive city in the country after London. Unfortunately for him, though, the best deals had all been done and he was looking to invest just as property prices were at their peak. Against Callum's advice he made a couple of poor decisions and ended up losing money. The loss hit him hard, his savings dwindled, and he found himself deep in debt.

Things got so bad that he was forced to sell his flat in Morningside at a loss and rent a flat off Callum. As if this wasn't bad enough, his father was diagnosed with cancer and told he only had months to live. Things were at crisis point and now suddenly ruin was knocking at the door. Desperate to turn things around, Gareth Cairns did the only thing he could under the circumstances: he joined the Labour Party.

This morning, he was again late for the weekly meeting of the parliament's Crime and Justice Committee, upon which he sat. It started every week at ten-sharp, but Gareth usually never showed up before quarter-past. He liked to squeeze in thirty minutes on the treadmill at the gym on a Monday morning, followed by another half an hour of relaxation in the sauna, to set him up for the week.

Anyway, he only sat on the Crime and Justice Committee because he was obliged to as part of his duties as an MSP.

As far as he was concerned, it was a complete waste of his time.

Which is why as soon as arrived at parliament, he went straight to the bathroom to check his hair and brush his teeth for the third time that morning. Only after doing that did he start making his way to the meeting.

He made his way up to the first floor via the back stairs rather than main staircase leading up from the atrium. He did so purposely to avoid the parliamentary reporters who hung around the atrium looking for people to interview. If Gareth was sure about anything it was that he wanted to remain in the background, invisible to scrutiny.

On he went up to the first floor, where he walked along the wood-panelled corridor that snaked around the building's circumference. All the way along it were various-sized meeting rooms and Gareth stopped outside Room-P2. The sign on the door read, Crime and Justice Committee: 10am-12pm. Pausing first to take a breath and prepare himself, Gareth turned the handle, opened the door and entered the fray.

Over to his usual chair he walked through a visage of grey suits and bland faces. The meeting was in progress and Gareth's presence drew disapproving looks.

Those in attendance were sitting around a large oval table with the obligatory glasses of water and notepads and pens lying in front of them, and Gareth closed the door behind him and walked smartly over to his chair, sensing the negative energy flowing in his direction as he did.

At that particular moment Tommy Anderson was in full flight with yet another of his barnstorming speeches. He was one of the Scottish Parliament's anomalies in that he was a strident socialist —- a man who by dint of his skills as an orator and a messianic commitment to the worst off in society, had managed to gain a certain amount of notoriety and publicity for his radical notions of justice and equality.

He lost no opportunity in telling all and sundry that this could only be achieved by taxing the rich and redistributing wealth to the poor. As far as most of his fellow MSPs were concerned, his very presence in parliament was damning evidence of the crippling deficiencies of proportional representation.

"…because unless we start to tackle the causes of crime — namely poverty and social exclusion — we will never eradicate it."

Anderson had come to the end of his contribution and sat down. At each place around the table a small microphone was connected to a sound system. It was activated with the push of a button. Tommy Anderson never bothered using the microphone himself, however, preferring instead to boom his message out in broad Glaswegian.

"So what's your proposal?" the chair of the meeting, Cathy Palmer, inquired, face betraying complete and utter befuddlement at the contents of the speech she'd just heard.

Anderson cleared his throat. "My proposal is that we commission a study into the links between poverty and crime. And that based on the findings of this study, we devise specific and concrete policies to eradicate poverty with the aim of eradicating crime."

Raised eyebrows and expressions of derision met Anderson's proposal. Immediately Donald Caruthers, Tory MSP, shot his hand up.

"Donald?" Cathy Palmer nodded in his direction, inviting him to speak.

"I strenuously disagree," Carruthers began, spitting the words out with unalloyed disgust. "To suggest that the issues of crime and poverty are linked is deeply offensive to me and, I am sure, to the vast majority of decent law abiding citizens in low income communities. There is scant evidence to support any such link, and this committee should not be beguiled into commissioning a study that would purport to find one."

"When was the last time you ever spoke to anyone from a low income community?" Anderson interjected with a sneer.

"All contributions through the chair please," Cathy Palmer chastised him.

Ann Reid, a Labour MSP from the adjacent constituency to Anderson in Glasgow, put her hand up and was invited to speak next.

"Speaking as a Labour MSP and a socialist myself," she began, "I…"

A loud guffaw emanated from the back of Anderson's throat as soon as the word 'socialist' left her mouth, filling the room with its derision and disrespect. In response, Ann Reid threw him a look.

"As a Labour MSP *and* a socialist," she continued assertively, "I do have a certain amount of sympathy for sentiments we've just heard expressed on this issue. However it is clearly beyond the competence of this committee to commission any such study and, further, to attempt to fashion legislation on the back of such a study. What I propose instead is..."

She continued to drone on and on —in a voice that was as flat and lifeless as her tits, it occurred to Gareth, watching her. In an effort to escape the stifling monotony he brought out his phone and typed out a quick message Callum nder the desk:

> *did 4 miles on tread this morning and going to do another 3 tonite.*

Upon pressing send he took a quick glance up to make sure nobody had noticed and put the phone back in his pocket.

The meeting was still in progress. Another longwinded

contribution was being delivered by another dull mediocrity in a cheap suit. Gareth had by now completely zoned out and wasn't even listening. He hated being at parliament and the possibility of pulling a sickie so he could leave early entered his head.

There was a debate being held in the chamber on the Executive's agriculture bill later but, fuck it, it would just have to take place without him. I need to get the hell out of Here. Maybe do some shopping, he mused. It's been over a week since I treated myself to that Armani jacket.

Yes, that's what I'll do, I'll suffer the rest of this fucking meeting then make my excuses and take off. Perhaps I should give Bill Mackie a buzz and see if he's around for lunch later. Be good to get an update on that new development of his out at Bonnyrigg. Made a good few quid in commission from his last one over in Corstorphine. Always helps to have connections at the Council. Getting planning permission can be such a bastard without them.

Last time I saw Bill he invited me to his box to watch the rugby at Murrayfield the next time there's a big game on.

Be lots of useful contacts at something like that. I need to make sure he remembers to hook me up.

Out again came the phone. Just as he began typing out his message to Bill Mackie, however, one arrived with a loud *'beep, beep!'* echoing in the room.

"So sorry," Gareth said sheepishly in response to the hostile eyes that immediately shifted onto him. "Family stuff," he went on. "Been waiting for news."

The meeting carried on where it left off and Gareth waited until everyone's attention had left him before reading the incoming message. It was a reply to his original message from Callum.

> *Good, see u there. Just trying on jkts in HNicks. Armani or Farhi?*

Half a minute later, standing in one of the changing rooms at Harvey Nichols, Callum received Gareth's reply.

> *farhi. armani's bang out out of ideas this season*

Moments later Callum emerged from the changing room to be confronted by the sales assistant, who'd been waiting patiently.

"I'll take the Farhi please."

The sales assistant responded with a nod, before taking both jackets and leading the way over to the cash desk. At this time of the day the store was near deserted of customers was Callum's preferred time to shop. While the sales assistant folded and bagged the jacket, Callum lazily surveyed the shirts displayed on the table adjacent. They were by Paul Smith but none struck a chord and so he turned back to the cash desk just as the sales assistant rung up the price.

"Okay sir, your total today is five hundred pounds please."

Callum produced his Amex, placed it into the machine and typed in his pin. The sales assistant was tall and thin, stylishly dressed in a black two button suit and stiff white shirt. He had jet black hair and a deep tan, clearly painted on, and he moved and carried himself like a guy for whom the small details mattered.

Seconds later, the transaction completed, Callum removed and put it back in his wallet.

"Thank you," the sales assistant said with a practiced smile. "Your receipt's in the bag."

Callum swaggered the long way round to the down escalator, hoping to catch a glimpse of the hot chick who worked in the shoe concession, located in the far corner of the mens department. She was engaged to be married, he and the others had already ascertained but Callum liked to look and flirt with her regardless. And anyway, as he was fond of saying, you just never know with women who are spoken for — for all it takes is one argument, one fight, and, boom, they're open to offers.

He glided past the shoe concession where she worked, Harvey Nichols bag prominent by his side, but was disappointed to see that she wasn't there. This morning it was staffed by a short skinny guy with bad skin. Callum went over to him.

"Hi, how's it going?" he said. "Is Jane around by any chance?"

"It's her day off today," the skinny guy said through his nose.

"Oh well, no worries. If you could just tell her Callum dropped by to say hello."

"She'll be in tomorrow."

"It's okay, it's not important," Callum said. "I was just passing. I'll catch her next time."

Hitting the down escalator, he was disappointed to see that the escalator next to him was devoid of any attractive-looking women making their way up. To compensate he took advantage of the mirrored walls to have a good look at his reflection before reaching the ground floor.

The cosmetics department lay straight ahead, between the escalators and the main door, and he took a circuitous route on his way out in order to make himself as visible as possible to the gagggle of make-up girls behind the various counters.

On he went, passing through the big double doors, dutifully held open for him by the doorman. His phone started ringing as he was walking through St Andrew Square on his way to George Street, where he was parked.

"David, hi," Callum said into the phone. "So what did they bid in the end?...Half a million? Hmmm, not bad. What do you think?...Yep....Yes I agree. All right, let's take it. I'll pop round to the office in the morning to sign the paperwork….Nice one, David. Cheers."

And thus, with another property deal done, he put his phone away and continued on his way.

Callum Wilson was a man who liked to think of himself as self made, which was true if your idea of self made was an old man who owned shares in a mining company in Africa, a bank in St Lucia, and an oilfield in the Caspian Sea. Now, making his way along George Street, he brought his phone back out and punched out a number, buoyed with the news of his latest property deal.

The recipient of the call, Brian, was at that moment in his office with a patient way over on the other side of the city at Sighthill Health Centre, designed to cater to the health needs of the low income communities surrounding it. By rights, his phone shouldn't have been switched on during surgery. But on it was and he had no hesitation in interrupting his consultation to take the call.

"Excuse me one moment," he said to his patient as he reached across, picked up his phone and took the call.

"Hey Callum, what's going on?"

"Just thought you'd like to know," Callum told him as he

walked past The Dome on the opposite side of George Street, "Harvey Nicks have got their new season of Prada in. I just got myself a suit."

"Are they doing a navy blue this season?"

"There's a navy pinstripe you'd like. You out this weekend?"

"Of course I'll be out. Two button or one?"

"One and two button."

"What about coats? I need a raincoat." Brian saying this while smiling at his patient, Ms Hutchison, a woman in her late sixties with bad varicose veins and angina.

"I didn't notice any," Callum replied, stopping to look at his reflection in the window of a works van parked by the kerb. "How about a sunbed and a facial after the gym on Saturday? I'm feeling a bit run down."

"Okay, but I need to fit in some shopping as well," Brian said.

Ms Hutchison was in pain and began shifting uncomfortably in the chair.

"Look," Brian continued into the phone, "I'm with a patient. Let me call you later." He put the phone back down on the desk and returned his attention to his patient

"Okay, Ms Hutchison," he said. "What can I do for you today?"

"It's my legs, doctor. They're still giving me pain. I was wondering if there's anything you can do?"

"Ms Hutchison, we've already discussed this. You're on the waiting list for an operation that'll make your legs better. Until then, try and persevere with the painkillers I prescribed you last time. Okay?"

Tears now appeared in the poor woman's eyes.

"I know you're experiencing a lot of discomfort, but it shouldn't be too long before your operation. Try to relax and rest as much as you can."

"But…this pain. I don't know if I can cope."

She broke down and started to sob, bowing her head as in a plea for mercy.

"Look," Brian said, unable to bear it any more and turning to his computer. "Why don't we try different painkillers? Something a little stronger than what you're taking at the moment. It should help."

He quickly typed out a prescription, printed it out, removed it from the printer, signed it, and handed it over.

"Thank you doctor. I'm sorry, I didn't mean to cry…I just…"

"That's quite all right," Brian said, rising from his chair. "There's no need to apologise. I know how upsetting these things can be."

Brian walked across to the door and opened it for her she forced herself up out of the chair and began making her way out.

"You know where the dispensary is, don't you? It's just past reception on the right."

"Thank you," Ms Hutchison said, before shuffling out of the office.

"My pleasure," Brian replied. "I'll see you again soon."

He closed the door then walked over to the treatment table against the wall, lay down and put his feet up. Just as he was about to drift off to sleep the phone on the table started ringing.

Fuck, what now? Am I not entitled to a nap when I need one? I did five miles on the treadmill last night. I need some rest. Pissed off, he swung his legs off the table, raised himself up, walked over to his desk and picked up the phone.

"Okay…Yes, I know he's waiting. I was just about to call him in….All right, thanks for letting me know."

He ended the call, walked to the door, opened it and stepped out into the corridor. Along to the left was the waiting room. Brian walked along and popped his head round the door and called out, "Francis McGraw?"

Sitting in the waiting room were an old couple who appeared mere days away from a wooden suit, a middle aged man with what sounded very much like whooping cough, and a young methadone addict dressed in a tracksuit top, jeans and training shoes. In response to his name being called the meth addict stood up and followed the doctor into his office, whereupon Brian invited him to take the chair just vacated by Ms Hutchison. Great, Brian thought, just what I need before lunch — a junkie.

"Okay Francis, what can I do for you today?"

Sweat was running down the young man's face and his eyes were half shut. As he sat listening to him slur his words, Brian thought about the workout he had planned later. I want to beat Callum's record on the treadmill, he thought. I'm still a good twenty seconds behind him.

"Know what ah mean, doctor? I'm getting jellied oot ma nut cause ah'm no getting the meth ah need tae keep me level. Know what ah mean?"

Brian's attention was still elsewhere. I'm keen to try this new Thai place down in Stockbridge, he thought next. It's been getting rave reviews. I'll mention it to the guys. See if they fancy it this weekend.

"…Ma burd's fucked oaf wi' the bairn n aw, an ah cannae fuckin' cope. I feel like topping masel."
wonder if Julia's back from the South of France. I'll text her later. If she's back, I'll invite her to the Louise Bourgeois exhibition at the Fruitmarket Gallery. I've a feeling this might be its last week. After that I'll get her back to mine for some fun.

"So what dae ye think? Any chance ay an extra methadone prescription this week?"

## 3

*Only the shallow know themselves*

The Omni Centre on Greenside Place at the top of Leith Walk was an ugly glass fronted US-style leisure complex comprising a cineplex, various themed bars, fast food restaurants, offices, and in the basement a state of the art gym. The gym was called Holmes Place and was geared towards an upscale professional clientele with the facilities and membership fees to match. Day and night they could be found in here working to improve and maintain bodies and physiques in which they set such great store.

This they did with regular gym sessions, spinning classes, yoga, pilates, and a host of other workouts. Designer gym outfits were obligatory, as were for women make-up and due attention to hair and nails. For the guys it was all about making sure the colour scheme was right, that shorts were worn just above the knee to show off a little bit of quad and that training shoes were the latest on the market. In life, after all, it's crucial you get your priorities right.

On this Monday evening, just before seven, the boys were in the middle of another hard session. They were running on treadmills lined up next to one another, and the energy created sat somewhere between electric and nuclear. Callum held the record for the best time and had done for a couple of months now, but Brian had managed to close the gap to a mere ten seconds over the past few weeks. Gerry and Gareth were quite some way behind those two but remained unconcerned, as their main priority was the ongoing rivalry with each other.

Tonight they were really going for it, legs and arms pumping and all of them covered in sweat. As soon as he reached the four mile mark, Callum upped the pace, increasing the level on his machine to 12. Brian followed suit, determined not to let him streak ahead and their breathing became audible as the pain and exertion started to bite.

Gerry and Gareth were both sitting at level-9 and working just as hard. The front of their respective machines had begun to vibrate, their feet striking the base of the treadmill with a clatter-clatter, and their upper bodies shook as they struggled to keep the pace up. Callum further upped the ante in his competition with Brian when he pushed the pace up to level-13 with half a mile to go. Come on, push it, he thought. Push it. Show them who the man is. Come on, Callum. Come on, son.

Bastard, Brian thought, running on the treadmill alongside him. Think you're going to beat me? Not tonight. Tonight I'm going to kick your arse. And he too pushed his level up a notch. If anything the rivalry between Gerry and Gareth was fiercer, especially when Gareth moved up to level-10. There, he thought, beat that arsehole.

Gerry was running out of gas and quickly. Consequently when Gareth increased his pace he started to panic. Fuck! he screamed silently, stealing a quick look at Gareth's panel and seeing him pulling away. Gerry, you have to do something. You have to do something! You're getting beat! He's beating you!

With no other option available he pushed his speed up to level-12 in a last ditch attempt to call Gareth's bluff. He's knackered, Gerry tried telling himself. Hang on, just hang on, he'll slow down! He can't keep this up, he can't! Gerry, hang on, hang on!..Gerry!...

But Gerry was going too fast to hang on; his legs were numb, the feeling in them draining away as the muscles struggled to cope with the build-up of lactic acid, and he began pumping his arms furiously in an effort to compensate.

With his jaw clenched tight, his features contorted and turning redder by the nano-second, he was in trouble, running and pumping and blowing in a desperate attempt to outlast Gareth. They were constantly looking over at one another's instrument panel to monitor the distance they each had left. Finally, Gareth's right hand moved over his panel. Yes, Gerry thought, he's going to slow down! Yes!

But then suddenly, like a new born calf, Gerry's legs gave way and he collapsed forward with an almighty bang. Luckily he managed to throw his hands forward and catch the safety rail that ran along the front of the treadmill, else he would've been looking at a fractured skull. Gareth reached over and hit Gerry's red emergency stop button, bringing his treadmill to an immediate stop. Brian and Callum only had seconds to go before reaching the five mile mark and kept going. Gareth thought briefly about stopping but decided better of it and kept going also. He only had another minute to go and Gerry could wait.

Gerry was more embarrassed than hurt by the fall, and he quickly stood up and away from the machine in an effort to attract as little of the wrong kind of attention as possible. It was too late. Running over came two members of staff who'd heard the commotion from across the other side of the gym.

"Are you all right? Are you hurt?" the female instructor asked Gerry solicitously in a voice loud enough for people in the immediate vicinity to overhear.

"Come on, let's get you over to the first aid station," the young bloke said, grabbing Gerry by the elbow and starting to guide him away.

"Leave me alone," Gerry barked at them, causing the two of them to step back in surprise. "I'm fine," he went on in a calm voice, realising he'd just lost control and quickly reining himself back in. "I'll be fine. It was nothing."

"Look," the young bloke began, "perhaps…"

"I'm fine, Gerry spat at him through gritted teeth. "Okay? I'm okay."

The instructors shrugged and backed off. As soon as they did Gerry hobbled across the gym to the water fountain over by the wall. He did so conscious of numerous pairs of eyes following him. Much to his consternation, many of them belonged to members of the opposite sex. This was not good. This was not good at all.

Following their five miles on the treadmill, which tonight Callum completed in 38 minutes and 34 seconds, the boys headed over to the free weight area to pump some iron. Tonight they were working their shoulders and arms and began the workout super-setting dumbbell lateral raises with shoulder presses on the machine.

They used relatively light weights in all their exercises. Not for them a pumped up, overdeveloped physique. No, the athletic physique of an Olympic athlete is what they were looking to achieve. Gerry, eager to expunge the humiliation of his debacle on the treadmill, kicked things off by hurtling headlong into the first superset with the determination of a madman. The others watched as he grunted and growled, forgetting completely in the process the women working out close by.

It got so bad that Callum decided he would need to have a word with him later.

Half an hour later, the workout over, all of the guys apart from Brian were relaxing. Brian had taken off straight after the workout as tonight was his night with the kids. The others were intent on a sauna and massage before heading home, and right now they were in the sauna basking in the afterglow of a hard workout, each naked apart from a white towel tied round the waist, luxuriating in the heat in silence.

At a certain point, Gerry piped up. "I think I could do another inch on my arms."

Callum opened his eyes and looked at him. "Maybe. Your delts still overshadow them a bit."

"They're fine," Gareth said. "Just stick to your diet."

"What do you mean?" Gerry said, instantly triggered. "Are you saying I need to lose weight?"

"This time last year you were leaner," Gareth replied.

"I'm still leaner than you."

"No you're not."

"Yes I am," Gerry said, before turning to Callum for support. "Callum?"

Callum sighed. "Come on guys, not again?"

Gareth said: "I just beat you on the treadmill again, didn't I? Or was I imagining it when you went over on your arse?"

"I lift heavier weights than you."

"Sometimes."

Gerry chuckled in an attempt to mask the fact that Gareth was getting to him. "You're insane," he said. Then, turning to Callum once again, he continued, "The man's insane."

That was it for Gareth, the final straw, and he stood up. "All right," he announced, "let's have a posedown. Callum, you can judge."

Gareth had just taken both Gerry and Callum by surprise. "What?" Gerry said. "Come on…"

"So you admit it then," Gareth said, cutting him off. "I'm leaner and fitter than you. Good, thank you. Now, moving on, how about that new Thai place in Stockbridge Brian suggested for this weekend?"

But Gerry wasn't having that and stood up as well. "Let's go," he said as he made for the door.

"Come on, Gerry" Callum pleaded. "He's just winding you up."

Gerry opened the door, ducked his head down and stepped out, before turning round to reply. "No he's not. He thinks he's better than me. Well, let's find out once and for all, shall we? The mirror doesn't lie."

Gareth followed him out of the sauna with a smug grin on his face, leaving Callum to contemplate the role of honest broker yet again. Here we go, he thought, standing up and fixing his towel before heading out behind them. Here we fucking go.

Moments later, in the middle of the changing room, in front of one of three large full length mirrors, Gerry and Gareth were standing side by side hitting poses in the style of competitive bodybuilders.

Behind and to the side, Callum looked on, appropriately mortified.

Gerry and Gareth were oblivious and continued to hit poses in the mirror with the intensity and seriousness of men who were engaged in mortal combat. This was a matter of honour, of bragging rights, and neither was about to give way.

They would rather wear a suit out of H&M before doing that, which was really saying something considering that the mere mention of H&M in this company was akin to the most egregious blasphemy.

On it went. This embarrassing spectacle. On and on.

## 4

*In nothing do men more nearly approach the gods than in giving health to men*

It was late, approaching midnight, and Brian was driving through deserted city streets. This was his week being on-call and normally he'd be lucky if he had to deal with more than two or three calls on any given night. However tonight he'd already been called out six times and was now on his way home after visiting his latest patient in Broomhouse on the western outskirts of the city.

Annoyed at being so busy, he decided to make one quick phone call and then turn his phone off. He wasn't supposed to turn his phone off; he was meant to remain available throughout the night in case anyone needed an emergency call out. But he was going to switch it off anyway, and thus the decision made he put the driver's side window down in an effort to purge from his system the squalor he'd just left behind in Broomhouse.

It had taken him nine long years of studying and training to become a GP and since then he'd been practicing for four years. In that time how much had changed. Entering university to study medicine, he was a young man filled with the idealism of those who believe they could and should try to make a difference. Back then he felt an affinity with the poorest and most vulnerable in society, imbued with a sense of moral outrage at the inequality and injustice that blighted the lives of so many at home and was the scourge of the developing world. In entering medicine, Brian was following in the footsteps of his parents, both doctors themselves, and a grandfather who'd helped to pioneer advances in the treatment of pulmonary fibrosis.

His grandfather passed away not long after Brian entered university, delighted to have lived long enough to witness his only grandson pick up the baton. As for his parents, they were especially proud of their son's commitment to medicine as a way of promoting social justice. They'd both spent many years working in the developing world; meeting one another in India doing just that. To hear their son pledge to follow their example had been a validation of everything they held dear.

All through university Brian never wavered from this worldview and upon graduation signed up with an NGO to do voluntary work overseas. He felt he would gain much more invaluable experience doing that than he would working in a hospital at home surrounded by the luxury of modern technology and medicines.

So off he went to Africa —Ethiopia, to be precise — joining a medical mission that was hopelessly underfunded and under-resourced as it fought a losing battle to stem an epidemic of infant deaths from preventable disease and hunger.

Returning to Scotland two years later, he was man transformed by the experience. This transformation, though, was negative rather than positive in scope; his idealism and sense of vocation eroded as a result of having been submerged in a sea of hopelessness, suffering and unremitting despair.

He went to work on attachment at the city's Royal Infirmary, putting in the final two years of training required to qualify as a GP. Day in and day out he assisted the doctors treat patients suffering the entire gamut of medical complaints. In the process he found it impossible not to compare the relative luxury and comfort of life at home with the absolute poverty of sub-Saharan Africa. By the time he finally qualified his outlook had changed to the point where the last shred of idealism he possessed had been replaced by a jaundiced view of the society of which he was a product. It was view that had remained with him throughout the intervening years, with the end result was that for him, now, the only thing worthwhile about being a doctor was a salary that more than compensated for having to deal with human detritus in places like Broomhouse.

Speaking of which, he still had his phone call to make.

"Hey darling, it's me. Were you sleeping?...Yes babes I know it's late, but I'm just on my way home from work and wondered if you fancied coming over. I'm off tomorrow and I was thinking we could spend some time together....You know I do....What's that? You're getting fanny flutters just hearing my voice again? Haha, that's nice....You know how much I like being with you....Great. See you in say half an hour-forty minutes?...Okay sexy, see you soon. Bye...Bye."

Brian put the phone back down on the passenger seat, breathed in a lungful of cold night air and put his window back up. He was feeling better, like himself again, and hitting the Western Approach Road into the city centre, he hit the accelerator.

Sharon Bradley was five-eight with short brown hair and unfortunate teeth. Originally from Glasgow, she ran a hairdressing salon in Corstorphine on the west side of Edinburgh. Brian met her just as she was close to finalising a bitter divorce from her ex— a former Scottish rugby international who'd managed to parlay his first career into a second as a media pundit.

Out celebrating the divorce and her success in fleecing he ex with a few friends in the bar of the Raeburn Hotel in Stockbridge on this particular night, Sharon was wired on coke when she gave Brian a memorable blowjob in one of the cubicles in the mens. When she texted him a picture of a lobster two days later, he didn't know whether to laugh or cry. Regardless, Brian had been banging her every few weeks since in what had proved a convenient arrangement for both.

The only downside when it came to Sharon was that the conversation was invariably limited. On her phone Zara's website and the Sun newspaper horoscope page were hegemonic, confirming that intelligence was not her strong suit. Indeed, to describe this woman's brain as being lighter than a meringue would be to render an injustice to the meringue.

But that was all right because where sex was concerned, this particular woman was as dirty as a dug's arse.

She duly arrived at Brian's as arranged and they settled down in his sitting room with a bottle of champagne — M&S own brand stuff of the decidedly cheaper variety, as befitting both Sharon Bradley and the occasion.

Tonight she had on a pair of tight jeans, short leather jacket, vest top and red heels. Her skin was golden brown from regular sunbed sessions and glistened with lotion, and even though she may have put on a bit of timber since the last time they met, sitting alongside her on his leather two-seater with the scent of her perfume filling his senses, Brian's cock was verily bursting through his trousers — with the blue pill he'd popped in the car earlier kicking in nicely.

Before long they were kissing and soon enough she had her hand inside his fly, pulling him off. Brian responded by lifting her top and sucking her tits. On his mind was her tongue licking his balls. Sharon's blowjobs were definitely up there and Brian's loins tingled in anticipation as he ran his hands up and down her body and back and forth over her stomach, making the sign of the cross as if blessing that which he was about to receive.

Finally — and, oh God, thankfully — she leaned over and gently took him in her mouth, causing him lurch back with a groan.

"Naughty boy, you want me to suck you dry, don't you?" she teased while running her tongue up and down his shaft.

"Oh fuck yes."

"Have you missed me?" This while wrapping her tongue around the head.

"You know I have, baby. You know I have."

"How much have you missed me?" Now licking his balls.

At just after eight the next morning, Sharon awoke and began caressing Brian next to her until he also stirred awake. She was horny and eager for him to fuck her again. He duly obliged, spreading her legs and entering a vagina which by now was as slack as a clown's pocket.

Then, suddenly, he stopped.

"What's wrong?" she snorted, lying under him panting like a dog and sweating like a horse. "Why have you stopped?"

"What day's this?"

"What? Thursday. Fuck sake, why?"

Brian rolled off of her and got up. "I've got to go," he declared on his way into the en-suite, switching on the light and turning the shower on, hot water whooshing and filling the bathroom up with steam within seconds.

"Go where?" she called through from the bedroom. "You said you were off today."

"I take my kids to school on a Thursday," he called through from the shower. "Sorry, I completely forgot."

"So you're just going to leave me lying here — in this state?"

"You've got two hands, darling."

"Fuck you!" Sharon Bradley roared at him, before jumping up out of bed and starting to gather her things. She was furious and her fury was exacerbated by the sound of him humming in the shower. "Wanker!" Spitting this while furiously pulling her jeans on.

Brian ignored her and continued to hum and sing away, enjoying the revitalising effect of the hot water on his body.

"This is the last time you'll use me like this; the last fucking time." Now putting on her shoes, sitting on the edge of the bed fastening the straps.

"Don't you call me again — ever!"

Finished putting on her shoes, she got up, grabbed her keys and bag from the side of the bed, and headed for the door.

"Arsehole!" she called back at him as she went.

"Don't slam it please."

She did precisely the opposite, before clum-clumping down the stairs on her way out of the building.

Fifteen minutes later, Brian climbed into his car and started off for his ex-wife Gail's house. She lived with their kids — one boy and one girl age 6 and 8 respectively — in the three-bedroom bungalow on Ravelston Dykes the two of them bought together when things were still good. This part of the city was affluent, safe and, just as importantly, in close proximity to some of the Edinburgh's elite private schools. A long street that ran the best part of a mile, Ravelston Dykes was bordered by trees its entire length, concealing the well appointed and spacious houses of its upper middle class residents. Despite being adjacent to the city centre, the dominant sound in this part of the city was not that of traffic but of birds singing and chirruping, adding further to Ravelston's attraction.

At this time in the morning, midweek, the street was colonised by kids dressed in the uniform of one of the various private schools located in the vicinity, walking and skipping along in the company of mums, dads, or both, on their way to receive another day of expensive education; the bright
future that lay in store reflected in their confident demeanours.

Brian rolled up outside Gail's, parked, got out and walked through the swing gate and on up the path to the front door. The nature of the relationship they now enjoyed was such that he still retained his own key to the house. Using it to open the front door, in he went while calling out, "Hello, anybody home?"

"We're upstairs," a lilting female voice replied.

Gail and Brian originally met at university, where they were both doing a degree in medicine. The daughter of a Scottish Tory grandee, Gail entered medicine with the objective of qualifying as a consultant and moving to the States to enjoy the exorbitant fees medical consultants earned there.

They remained in touch even when Brian moved to Africa to work with a medical mission and Gail to the States to study at Harvard for the last two years of her degree. Even when Gail met Rob and entered a relationship with him, she and Brian continued to stay in touch. Rob hailed from a wealthy New York family and after dating Gail for only six months he proposed and she said yes. Thinking he would be delighted to hear the news, she emailed

Brian to let him know. In the same message she invited him over to the States to meet her now future husband; this on the understanding that though no longer intimately involved, the two of them would always remain friends. Brian was more than happy to accept and flew out to Boston a month later. Waiting to meet him at the airport were Gail and Rob, hand in hand as Brian emerged from customs and immigration into arrivals.

Rob, from the beginning, went out of his way to make Brian welcome and ensure he had a great time. He showed him around Boston, introduced him to a few of his friends from Harvard, and took him to a few bars; the two of them getting memorably drunk in an Irish pub one night and staggering home singing at the tops of their voices like a couple of old high school buddies.

Gail was delighted. Seeing her future husband and her ex getting along so well made her feel that life couldn't get better, what with Brian representing her past and Rob her future — with both, it seemed, merging naturally and harmoniously. She never imagined that life could be so straightforward and uncomplicated, and if she could she would've kept things exactly as they were during that first wonderful week of Brian's visit. Life, though, doesn't run so smooth. Instead it has the habit of removing the feet from under us at the very point at which we believe we've reached the summit of our heart's desires.

Creeping into both Gail's and Brian's consciousness as the days unfolded was the realisation they still loved each another, despite the time apart and regardless of the fact she was engaged to be married to another. It was an awful realisation, manifesting in a palpable awkwardness akin to the arrival of an unwelcome guest at a dinner party.

In consequence everything changed. Gone was the harmony and cosy togetherness of that initial week. In its place came tension and an energy-sapping confusion over what was occurring. No one was willing to confront the issue head on, each too afraid to initiate a full and frank discussion about what they were feeling and why, which only made matters worse.

Facing and broaching the issue was the logical thing to do. But logic and emotion have no place in the same room and the resulting tension manifested in bickering and arguing between Gail and Rob over various silly things — such as where to eat lunch, the use of a certain word or phrase during the course of a conversation, and so on.

Brian, on the sidelines, felt like his head was going to burst with the all the attendant stress. He was desperate to get Gail on her own to discuss matters, and she felt the same way. Rob, meanwhile, realising she was slipping from his grasp, clung on with everything he had, deluding himself that if he could just hold out until Brian left it would all blow over and everything would revert back to the way it was before. Of course, he tried consoling himself, it's only natural she might be attracted to an old flame. It happens to everyone at some point. An old flame represents the false comfort of familiarity. It's what we do — we like to wallow in nostalgia for the past as a way of distracting us from the uncertainty symbolised by the future. This is what Gail's doing now, wallowing in the past.

But it was no use, the spell has been broken and finally, inevitably, it all came spewing out. That it did the night before Brian was due to leave only made it all the more dramatic.

During dinner that evening the conversation was even more strained than it had been hitherto, with a palpable sense of a looming reckoning present. It duly arrived after Brian said goodnight and went upstairs to bed, whereupon Gail and Rob got into a big fight. Drunk after sinking a bottle of red and two scotches and soda, Rob accused Gail of still being in love with her ex.

Instead of denying it, as he was hoping for dear life she would, Gail started to cry and with Rob still pushing her admitted that, yes, she was still in love with Brian. Pain and anger instantly flooded Rob's insides like a cascading mountain of water bursting through a dam. With Gail's confession ringing in his ears, Rob marched from the dining room and on up the stairs. Brian was in bed reading when he came bursting through the door.

"Piece of shit!"

Before Brian got a chance to react Rob was on top of him, flailing away with his fists. They proceeded to fall off the bed and were rolling around on the floor when Gail appeared, screaming at them to stop, stop it this instant, as she watched her entire come apart right in front of her eyes.

Brian finally managed to overpower and pin Rob down.

"What the hell do you think you're doing?!"

Rob just lay there, inert. The fight had been sapped out of him; rage replaced by pain in the knowledge that he'd lost - lost Gail. Yes, it was over and nothing would ever be the same.

Brian left to go back to Africa via the UK the following day and Gail moved out of the house shortly after. The wedding was cancelled and aware that all her friends in America were mutual friends she'd shared with Rob, Gail quickly decided that she could no longer remain in Boston and be happy and so returned to Scotland. She didn't immediately return to Brian, though. No, she wasn't yet ready for that — not after the fractious nature of the break-up with Rob. She needed space, time on her own, and Brian was happy to oblige while his time in Africa wound down towards its end and his own return to Scotland.

But for all that, there was an unspoken understanding between them that eventually they would be together. In this, in the way their relationship had been rekindled, it seemed fate had taken a hand. When finally they did so, they seemed the perfect couple; Gail soon falling pregnant with their first child and Brian just embarking on his career as a fully fledged GP.

When it all came to an end five years later none of their friends could believe it. By now they had two beautiful children, nice house, two cars, and enjoyed regular holidays abroad — in sum, everything a young couple and family could possibly want. Boredom, that most unsettling of emotions, set in regardless, acting as a corrosive that gradually ate away at their bond.

As every couple does when they find themselves in this situation, initially they refused to acknowledge there was a problem, denying it both to each other and to themselves. It'll pass, is what they each thought initially and delusionally. It's just a passing phase, nothing to get worked up about, merely part and parcel of married life.

But rather than pass, the rift between them continued to grow, until it became a chasm impossible to bridge. Brian yearned to be single again, to enjoy the fruits of the years of the hard work and dedication he'd put in to qualify as a GP. Nights in front of the television with Gail, the kids tucked up in bed, he found increasingly enervating. As for sex, it became near non-existent, what with Gail constantly tired from looking after two toddlers and hardly ever in the mood, and what with Brian exhuasted after a long shift at the medical practice dealing with abject misery. All in all, married life hadn't turned out to be what they expected and as time went by it was something neither of them wanted anymore.

The split, when it came, was amicable, shorn of the bitterness and acrimony that commonly accompanies marriage breakdowns. Both agreed that the friendship they shared was more important than the intimacy and that in order to protect their kids from undue stress they needed to end things like two responsible adults. This they did and ever since had enjoyed a platonic relationship that succeeded in leaving the kids as near to unaffected as possible in circumstances.

"Hiya pal," Brian greeted his boy at the top of the stairs, stroking the top of his head. "What are you doing up here then, eh? You getting ready for school? Where's your sister? Is your sister with mummy? Come on, let's go and find them."

He took Harry by the hand and walked with him along the landing towards the bathroom where Gail was busy helping Lucy wash her face and hands with a wet cloth, both of which were covered in makeup.

"How's it going?" Brian asked his ex.

"Lucy decided she wanted to wear lipstick to school this morning," Gail told him. "I've had a fair old time trying to get it off.

"Haven't I, eh?" she said affectionately to their daughter, standing beside her mum in front of the sink smiling knowingly as Gail continued to wipe her face and hands with the cloth.

"Come on Daddy," Harry instructed, "we have to go."

"Kids that love school," Brian quipped. "The world's gone mad."

Gail emerged from the bathroom with Lucy and Brian led the way downstairs with Harry. At the bottom of the stairs Gail walked along the hall into the kitchen, retrieved their packed lunches and placed them in their satchels. Watching her while enjoying the warm glow of domesticity for the first time in a long time, Brian said,

"Why don't we do something this weekend? We could take the kids to see a movie."

"I can't this weekend."

Brian processed her answer.

"How is Graham anyway?"

Graham was an architect with his own firm in Glasgow and Gail had been seeing him for the past six months. Brian had come across him two or three times at Gail's — this when he'd been there either dropping off or collecting the kids — and on each occasion tension had been palpably present. Gail seemed happy enough, though, and according to her he was good with the kids, so fair enough.

"He's fine," Gail told him in response

"Daddy, come on," Harry said, pulling him.

"You'd better go before he pulls your arm off," Gail said.

"All right, you win," Brian said to his son. "Come on then guys, off we go."

He opened the front door and the kids erupted from the house, racing headlong up the path to the gate like a couple of unguided missiles. Brian followed them, smirking at their antics as Gail watched their departure from the front door. The children were the most important thing in both their lives and occasionally Brian asked himself why they weren't still together?

But then he remembered that it wasn't so much that their marriage had been a mistake, as the fact that the very concept of marriage itself was a mistake. This, at least, was the conclusion he'd arrived at. Yes, he thought, the reason he and his ex got on so well now was precisely because they weren't together.

## 5

*Lead us not into temptation, Lord, but deliver us from evil*

Saturday afternoon and Harvey Nichols is heaving. Four floors of designer clothes, jewellery, cosmetics and accessories — the best and most expensive that money can buy — and there's no shortage of customers. In they come, exchanging a smile with the doorman as they do, entering a bubble of luxury and consumerism, a veritable Aladdin's cave packed with everything the lifestyle and celebrity magazines dictate you should have else be consigned to the status of a nobody, which for such people was a tantamount to a fate worse than death.

Cosmetics and perfumes? All spread out in front of you on the ground floor alongside ladies handbags.

Straight ahead lies the escalator taking you up to three floors of designer this, that and the other. Menswear on first floor is home to Gucci, Armani, Prada, Paul Smith,

Burberry, Hackett, Stone Island and many many more, all of it in front of your feasting-yearning eyes.

Need a new pair of jeans? Look no further, we've got it all, every style, cut, colour and wash; and at three hundred quid a pop guaranteed to make you stand out and garner those admiring looks and compliments that are as vital to your existence as oxygen. How about a pair of shoes? Well, none of your mass produced High Street garbage in this establishment — no, the shoes on sale here are of the highest quality, befitting only people of the highest quality. Try a pair and see for yourself. Feel the quality of the leather. These shoes are made to last and we only ever stock a few pairs in each style.

What's that? Do we take Visa? Of course we do — Visa, Mastercard, Amex, we take them all. That's it, just stick your card in the machine there, punch in your pin and you're all good. Oh and by the way — here, just for you — a ticket to our promo party night, guaranteed to be packed with Edinburgh's beautiful people. Just think of the fun you'll have with your free glass of champagne, discounts, live music and other attractions. Don't thank us, you're more than welcome. Thank you for your custom. Hope to see you again soon. Enjoy your purchase.

The elevator arrived at Harvey Nichols restaurant and cafe on the fifth floor with its usual perky *ding!*, the doors slid open and out they came — Brian, Gareth, Gerry and Callum —a vision of insouciance with their Harvey Nichols bags containing that week's purchases dangling by their sides as they proceeded to saunter through the place, feeling the eyes being raised from plates in response to their arrival, relishing every second of the attention as they made their way to their usual table (always reserved of course) by the window. Immediately upon seeing them Pierre made his way over with a big beaming smile on his face, bringing with him four menus.

"Good afternoon gentlemen," he said while placing the menus down on the table. "Nice to see you all again."

"Hello Pierre," Callum said, as he sat down along with the others, "how's you?"

"I'm great. Always better after seeing you guys."

"Pierre," Gareth said, "you're wasted here. You should be a diplomat with that charm."

"Diplomat, moi? My God, if I went into a room representing my country, we'd get invaded —again."

The boys all laughed.

"Very good," Brian said. "If not a diplomat then a comedian for sure."

"Absolutely," Callum agreed.

Pierre said, "Thanks, I shall take that as a compliment."

"It is," Gerry assured him.

Pierre cast his eyes over the bags they'd arrived with. "More shopping?"

"That, my French friend," Gareth said, "is the very definition of a rhetorical question."

Pierre stood there smiling, as much in amusement at Gareth's answer as with the anticipation of the business that was about to come the restaurant and bar's way from four of its most regular customers.

As he was thinking this, Gerry went into his bag and removed its contents in the shape of a cashmere sweater, black with a grey trim, which just cost him 550 quid.

"Pierre," Gerry said, opening it out, "what do you think? I thought this would look nice with jeans."

Like the aesthete he was, Pierre duly stepped back and adopted the pose of an art critic studying a new painting by an important artist, folding his arms and stroking his goatee-bearded chin with his right hand. "Hmm," he allowed, "who's it by?"

"Armani."

"Hmmm."

Gerry was crestfallen. Pierre's reaction wasn't the enthusiastic validation he'd been expecting.

"What's wrong?" Gerry said, eyes blinking rapidly like a man who's just been informed his missus is having an affair. "You don't like it? What don't you like about it; the colour, style — what?"

Pierre retained a furrowed brow for a few more seconds before breaking into a smile.

"Ah…I had you, eh?" he said, laughing.

Gerry's face burned with embarrassment, exacerbated by the laughter emanating from the others at the table.

"You should've seen your face," Callum declared, followed by a loud guffaw. "You don't like it?" Gareth said next, mimicking Gerry in a high pitched voice. "What don't you like about it; the colour, style — what?" And then more laughter, so loud it attracted the attention of people at adjacent tables.

"All right, all right," Gerry said, "it wasn't that funny."

Brian was the only one who'd used the time to take a look at the menu. "What do you recommend today, Pierre?"

"The fillet-mignon is especially good," came Pierre's reply. "Chef has done it in a beef sauce, using his own recipe. Try it."

The boys thought about it a moment, exchanged a look, and as in a rehearsed response looked up at Pierre and, in unison, said, "Salad."

"Salad again, okay, "Pierre confirmed. "And to drink? Champagne?"

The boys smiled, closed their menus and Pierre collected them. "Pierre, it's official, Callum said. "You're a genius."

"Oh yes, I know," Pierre said with a smile, before taking his leave.

"Those two girls at the table over there," Gerry said, having cast his eyes around the restaurant. "Didn't we end up at a party with them one night a couple of months back?"

"Not me," Gareth said, looking over. "I don't go to those kind of parties."

The others concurred with Gareth's sentiment in the form of a knowing smile.

"Why not invite them to join us?" Callum said, joking.

"Are you out of your mind?" Gareth came back.

Gerry, though, had taken Callum's suggestion to heart and on impulse got up from the table and made his way over.

"What the hell's he doing?" Brian said, watching him go. Callum shook his head in disdain. "He's lost it. The man has definitely lost it."

Gareth could only agree. "Three o'clock on a Saturday afternoon. How desperate can you get?"

And then, as if from nowhere, *she* appeared for the first time.

Five-ten, Latin, tall and slender, her long black hair, translucent and alive, travelled all the way down her back, while her brown eyes shone like beacon. She walked through the restaurant, being led to her table by Pierre, emitting the aura of a woman who knew things, dressed in a simple ensemble comprising a plain white shirt, fitted blue jeans, and knee-length leather boots.

Here indeed was a vision feminine beauty and sensuality such as Edinburgh had never witnessed, and the moment she arrived the atmosphere underwent a palpable transformation, with the energy in the place immediately flowing in her direction as if guided there by some supernatural force.

Pierre guided her to a reserved table slap-bang in the middle of the restaurant, where she sat down and took the menu from him with a smile. Not once did she betray any sign of being aware of the thirty or so sets of eyes now studying her. She was aware if it of course, but by now she was more than used to this sort of attention and had learned to block it out.

Her name was Tania and she was here by herself. That she was by herself just seemed wrong, all wrong, flying in the face of everything that was holy, thereby adding mystique to the kind of sex appeal that was beyond what most watching her had ever witnessed outwith the pages of fashion magazines.

Callum and Gareth stared open-mouthed as she took her seat. As for Brian, over him had come a feeling of such intense attraction he was finding it difficult to breathe properly.

"My God," Callum declared to no one and everyone.

"Who the hell is that?" Gareth asked. It was a question directed as much to himself as the others.

"I don't know, but I'm about to find out," Brian announced, before getting up from the table and heading in her direction.

He left the table almost at the same time as Gerry returned from the other side of the restaurant. Gerry had been so engrossed in conversation with the two girls at their table he hadn't noticed the presence of greatness in the form of the Latin queen who'd just arrived in their midst.

"Well," he began with a cheesy grin, "all I can say is it looks like I've scored. They wouldn't give me their number, but they…" He stopped in mid-sentence upon noticing that the attention of Gareth and Callum was riveted elsewhere. Following their eyes, he noticed Brian making his way through the place for the first time.

"Where's he off to?"

"Heaven," Callum answered.

Gareth nodded in agreement, and without taking his eyes away said to Gerry, "Sit down. This could be interesting."

As soon as Brian reached Tania's table, he froze. He'd ran over a dozen opening lines on the way over but now that he'd arrived his brain had liquefied, reducing him to standing at her table like a child who couldn't find its parents.

Feeling his presence, Tania looked up from her menu. "Yes?" she said in an accent that had New York stamped all over it. "Can I help you?"

"Eh…well…"

"Would you like to sit down?" she asked, pointing to the vacant seat on the other side of the table. Brian duly sat down with his stomach spinning like a washing machine and his head not far behind.

"Do you have a name?"

"Brian."

It took as much effort as he could muster to get this out, but now that he had he felt better and began to relax.

"Nice to meet you, Brian," she remarked. "I'm Tania."

And now it came, everything that Brian wanted to say. "You're beautiful. I mean…" A sudden movement of his right hand as the words left his mouth succeeded in knocking over an empty water glass. "Shit, I'm sorry, I…"

"Don't worry about it," Tania said. "There was nothing in it."

Ronald the head waiter appeared. He knew Brian, Brian knew him, but now was not the time to intrude with pleasantries and Ronald kept his attention focused on Tania.

"Something to drink madam?" he inquired.

It was at this precise moment that Tania's gaze moved over Brian's left shoulder to the table across the other side of the restaurant from where three meb were staring over, smiling and exchanging comments at the same time. In that instant she understood and in response smiled and said to Ronald, "Yes, can I have a bottle of Chablis please?" After pausing for effect, she continued, "Bring two glasses."

Brian, looking on, felt like doing somersaults he was so excited. But then came the awful thought that perhaps he'd misunderstood and the other glass was not intended for arrived in his head. What if…? Fuck, what if she's waiting for someone?

"I'm sorry," he said, panicing at the prospect. "Were you expecting someone?"

Tania looked at him, through him, eyes shining as she drew out his obvious discomfort. Only when the resulting tension had reached breaking point did she smile.

"Yes…he's sitting across from me now."

Back at the table, meanwhile, the guys were agog.

"Don't tell me he's actually going to pull?" Gareth said.

"She's unbelievable," Callum said.

"I'd use her shite for toothpaste," Gerry said.

Like parents who'd just caught their teenage son masturbating in the bath, Gareth and Callum regarded Gerry with reproach. He'd spoken without thinking and realising his mistake, came back sheepishly with, "Just something I heard from one of my clients."

Quickly moving his attention back to Brian and the Latin Princess in the middle of the restaurant, Gareth said, "He's going to fall in love with her."

"No, not Brian," Callum asserted. "He wouldn't do anything so idiotic as that." Then a pause, before: "Would he?"

"Idiotic, be damned," Gareth said. "Just look at her."

Gerry felt it was safe to speak again. "Just look at her? Just look at *him*. He looks like he needs a shite and a Sherman Tank at the same time."

Once again Gerry had brought the tone down to the level of the gutter, and once again Gareth and Callum hit him with a look of undisguised disapproval.

"Another client?" Gareth asked him, resulting in Gerry smiling apologetically at the same time as Callum made a mental note to have a word with him about the increasingly parlous state of his chat.

Ronald arrived back at Tania's table with the wine, two glasses and an ice bucket. With customary expertise, he placed a glass down in front of Tania and Brian respectively, placed the ice bucket in the middle of the table, produced a wine opener and uncorked the wine. He poured a smidgen into Tania's glass for her to taste.

"That's okay, just go ahead and pour please." Ronald did as instructed, filled Brian's glass too, placed the bottle in the ice bucket and took his leave.

"Cheers," Brian said, lifting his glass.

"Cheers," Tania responded, clinking his glass with hers and then taking a sip.

"Nice wine," Brian volunteered.

"Very nice," she agreed. "And also necessary given the week I just had."

"Really? Want to talk about it?"

"Na, I'd rather not if that's alright."

"No problem."

A brief pause ensued. It was broken by Tania. "Well, I sure wasn't expecting this."

"What were you expecting?"

"I was expecting a nice lunch, followed by a walk around this beautiful city, before returning to my hotel and spending the rest of the day catching up on work.

"Now look at me…seated across from a cute Scotsman sharing a bottle of wine."

Brilliant, just brilliant, Brian thought excitedly. Look at her. Absolutely fucking stunning. Thank you God — thank you, thank you, thank you!

"So tell me," Brian said, enjoying the effects of the wine, feeling relaxed and confident with the knowledge that this gorgeous woman sitting opposite liked him. "Do you each lunch by yourself often?"

"Only in places I don't have anyone to lunch with."

"First time in Edinburgh?"

"Indeed it is."

"Holiday? Sorry, I mean vacation."

"It's fine. I'm familiar with the European use of the word holiday as an antonym of our vacation. In answer to your question, I'm here on business.

"And you? Is Edinburgh home?"

"Yes."

"I can think of worse places to live."

"Where's home for you? Is that a New York accent I hear?"

"Well done."

"I have my moments."

Pierre arrived at the table. "Is everything okay here?"

"Pierre," Brian remarked, "as ever your timing is spot on."

"I'm happy you think so," Pierre said with a smile. "It's my job. Have you decided what you would like to order?"

"Jeez," Tania said, "we've been so engrossed in conversation, I completely forgot about food."

"I understand," Pierre replied solicitously. "Take as long as you need."

"If I was you," Brian told her, "I'd go for the fillet-mignon."

"Really?" Tania said, her interest piqued.

"It's my recommendation too," Pierre said.

"Okay, I'm sold. I'll have that with a side salad please."

"And how would madam like her steak?"

"Medium-rare."

"Very good," Pierre said. "And what about sir?" he asked Brian next.

"'Sir?' "Pierre, you know me better than your own wife."

"Yes," Pierre said, winking at Tania, "but she's not handsome like you."

Tania was tickled by Pierre's repartee and laughed.

"I'll just make do with my usual," Brian responded.

On that, Pierre smiled and departed

"I'm a doctor," Brian said, returning to the conversation.

"Really? Very impressive. I considered medicine as a career myself once. I've always found it fascinating.

Baby, I am going to fuck you, Brian thought, responding to the sudden tingling in his loins. You're so sexy and I am going to fuck you. "Yes," he said, continuing the conversation, "it certainly has its moments."

"So what is it you do?" he asked her in turn.

"Guess."

"Let's see. You're gorgeous and your work takes you all over the world." He paused then said, "Flight attendant?"

Tania laughed. "A flight attendant. No, I'm not a flight attendant. Not that there's anything wrong with being a flight attendant, of course, but that's not what I do "Not a bad guess though."

"What then?" Brian said. "I'm in suspense here."

"I work for an investment bank on Wall Street. I'm over here looking at new investment opportunities."

"Ah," Brian said. "Well, given the current climate I'm guessing this makes you about as popular as death right now."

"Actually, I'd say death just edges it."

The food arrived — Tania's fillet-mignon with a side saladand Brian's regular tuna salad — and they settled down to lunch.

Meanwhile, back at the other table, the guys were beside themselves with envy, their eyes still fixed firmly on Brian and the Latin princess sitting across from him, taking in the body language, the incontrovertible truth that he was in there.

"A minute to go in extra time in the final of the Champions League and he's just scored," Callum said.

"Christ, a football analogy," Gareth spat. "How tacky. Rugby's much more in keeping with men of quality."

"Don't worry," Gerry said. "we'll make up for it tonight."

"That's a bold statement coming from you," Gareth came back.

"Didn't you just see me at the table over there with those two hunnies?"

"Oh yeah? So where are they now?"

"They left to meet up with friends in George Street.

They've invited me to meet them later tonight at Potters."

"Potters Wine Bar on Thistle Street?"

"Yes," Gerry replied.

"That place went out of business two months ago."

Gerry's face collapsed along with his confidence, morale — everything. Gareth on the other hand had just won another victory in their perennial struggle for supremacy, and as such all was right in his world.

"Woe-woe, look, they're on the move," Callum announced, responding to the sight of Brian and Tania settling the bill. Ronald was at the table with the machine and Tania handed him a credit card. The fact she was paying only added to her charms as far as the guys were concerned.

"If he leaves with her, I want his lottery numbers," Gareth said.

"He won't," Gerry responded.

The bill was settled and Brian and Tania got up from the table and headed for the elevators. Waiting for one to arrive, Brian managed a quick look round and a wink.

"Superb," Callum said. "What a result."

"Brian is the man," Gareth affirmed. "No doubt about it."

## 6

*Love begins with an image; lust with a sensation*

They sat in the back of the cab, knees touching.

During the short journey from Harvey Nicks to the Balmoral Hotel at the east end of Princes Street, they hardly spoke — content, the two of them, to pass the time looking out the window at the hustle and bustle taking place in Edinburgh's city centre. Brian briefly thought about pointing out a few of the landmarks along the way, but then decided better of it and kept quiet. Better to save the conversation for when they got to the hotel and were alone.

The short journey to the hotel took them round the back of Princes Street via York Place then up Leith Street past John Lewis and the St James Centre right and the Omni Centre on the left, negotiating heavy traffic all the way. A clear day under a cloudless sky, and Edinburgh had never looked so majestic; its grand architecture and monuments combining with being in the company of this stunningly beautiful woman to leave Brian feeling close to euphoric. Finally, unable to remain silent, he ventured, "Majestic, isn't it?"

Tania looked at him. "Me or the city?"

He grinned. "Both."

Tania turned her head and looked out the window again. Brian took the opportunity to study her; he took in her long dark hair, dark skin, legs that were long and perfectly shaped, digesting every inch of her accompanied by a surge of anticipation at the thought of her naked. This, he knew, was going to be special.

As soon as the cab pulled up outside the Balmoral Hotel, the tartan-liveried doorman bounded down the small set of stone steps from the entrance, marched briskly across the pavement and opened the back door for them. As he did, Tania reached for her purse. Brian, however, beat her to it and leaned forward with a ten pound note, passing it to the driver through the gap in the grill and telling him to keep the change.

Tania walked across the pavement to the steps leading up to the hotel entrance. Before continuing up the steps, she stopped and turned to face Brian, behind her.

"Thanks for escorting me back to the hotel," she said. "It really wasn't necessary, but thank you all the same."

A complete change had come over her demeanour, her tone — over everything — resulting in Brian being thrown off balance.

"Eh…okay?"

"I can manage from here," she said.

"Right, well…am I going to see you again? I was going to ask you out for a drink tonight. There's place not too far from here on George Street…Tigerlily. It's…"

"I really don't think so," Tania said coldly, cutting him off in mid flow before turning and starting up the steps towards the hotel entrance. At the top of the steps she stopped and turned to face him again.

"Oh, and by the way," she said. "If it helps to boost your ego, feel free to tell your friends that we went back to my room and fucked like porn stars all afternoon."

"No…no, you've got it all wrong," Brian replied defensively. "It wasn't about that."

Ignoring his denial, she ended with, "I've always found weak men such a turn-off."

And with that Tania turned and walked on into the hotel, the doorman saluting her on the way in.

Brian remained at the foot of the steps, numb, oblivious to the doorman and the various passersby who'd just been privy to his humiliation; his euphoria at having been so sure of Tania's charms replaced by brutal disappointment. He briefly thought about following her into the hotel and attempting to turn the situation around. But then, kicking in, came common sense and, with it, the knowledge that that would be the worst thing he could do.

Brian continued standing at the bottom of the steps looking up at the hotel entrance for another few long seconds, struggling to come to terms with the rejection he'd just been dealt. Thought again about entering the hotel and trying to find her and attempting to recover the situation, but again managed to stop himself.

It was now that Brian's eyes now fastened onto the doorman. His name was Fred and stanging to the side of the entrance at the top of the steps, a smirk appeared on his face.

Brian retreated and walked to the corner where he joined the small cluster of people waiting to cross at the lights.

Finally, after what seemed like an interminable wait, the lights changed and he crossed over to the busy side of Princes Street, turning right and heading down Leith Street. His flat in the New Town was in walking distance. It was a nice day, warm with a cool breeze, and he decided to take a slow walk home to kill some time and process what had just happened. He'd switched his phone off as he was getting into the cab outside Harvey Nichols with Tania and now he switched it on again. Two messages arrived one after the other.

The first was from Callum:

>*lucky bastard. give me a bell later. we're dying to know how it went.*

The second was from Pam:

>*hi honey. out tonite? if so maybe i'll see u later? Let me know. Xx*

Brian thought about replying to Callum, but with nothing to report other than his humiliation, how could he? Shit, he would have to face them tonight. What will he tell them?

What *could* he tell them? Back there in the restaurant she was giving me all the signs; her body language, conversation, everything pointed in the same direction.

What the hell happened? Did I say something?

Then it came to him: Callum, Gerry and Gareth must have been staring over and she noticed. That's what she was getting at outside the hotel. They were looking over, she noticed them looking over, put two and two together and came up with five. Those three idiots fucked it for me. Christ, but she's beautiful. Not only beautiful, she's different. I don't know how to explain it, she just is. There's something about her.

The St James Centre loomed up beside him on his left like a monument to the disaster that befell architecture in the 1970s. Its functional lines and flat surfaces spoke of a decade in which people's expectations stretched to a shite job and a council house for life.

If you were lucky you took a summer holiday at a caravan site up north or down south; perhaps a weekend in Blackpool in addition to that if you were really pushing the boat out. You were happy with a black and white telly, which you had to put money in to operate, while there was never any thought of having a car. Even a phone was a luxury for most in those far off days. As for the better off, they had the pleasure of watching half their wages being confiscated by the government under a tax regime which gave new meaning to the term 'legalised theft'.

He passed John Lewis and continued on down Leith Street to the lights on York Place. Crossing, he meandered down Broughton Street with its arty cafes and trendy bars. Next, turning left onto Albany Street, he headed west in the direction of Abercrombie Place and home. He'd never been this smitten this quickly. Objectively, it could only be infatuation. His feelings at that moment, however, convinced him that what he'd just experienced with Tania, and for the first time in his life, was love at first sight.

So what now?

Arriving back at the flat, the option of returning home had suddenly lost its appeal. He stood outside his building paralysed with indecision, looking right then left before looking right again. Across the road was the private garden for the sole use of the residents of this exclusive New

Town address. For a few moments he considered taking himself over there to sit on a bench and ponder things.

Na, he thought, too bloody depressing. I'll only end up disappearing up my own arse.

I know, I'll head back into town for a spot of shopping. Maybe get that Daytona I've had my eye on at Hamilton & Inches; Brian thinking this as he started walking, experiencing a warm glow in his breast similar to that produced by a good malt. Yes, and maybe I'll also have a quick look in Hawes & Curtis while I'm at it for a new suit.

And so, suitably fortified, on he marched up Hanover Street in the direction of George Street, enjoying the breeze that was blowing against his face. By the time he arrived at George Street, gone was the moping, self-pitying, lovestruck specimen of before. Returning like an old friend with a warm welcome was the confident, self-assured man he was, salivating at the prospect of another shopping fix and focused on this and this alone the closer he came to his first port of call — Hamilton & Inches — one of the city's, nay nation's, premier jewellers.

Hamilton & Inches' range of men's watches and timepieces was beyond comparison, and Brian's heart verily pounded with excitement as he approached the store's window to feast on the Cartier, IWC, Breitling and Rolex watches that were on display. The fact he possessed five already — a Rolex Submariner and Datejust, Cartier dress watch, Panerai and a Breitling — was irrelevant. He needed, wanted, desired, coveted another watch and he was going to have one. And not just any watch either. Oh no, he was going to have that one there, the stainless steel Rolex Daytona with the champagne face.

Look how beautiful it is. My God I really do need it; I really do need it now. At just over seven grand it's a snip too, especially when you consider that to buy a Rolex is to buy an investment. Yes, thinking about it there's absolutely no good reason not to buy it. I haven't had anyone pass a compliment on my timepieces for a while now, and there is no surer a sign that you need a new one than that.

Brian pressed the bell by the side of the glass doors, the door buzzed open, and into the shop he went, passing the usual pleasantries with the doorman in the process. It didn't take long for him to ascertain he was the only customer in the place; the store at that precise moment was as quiet and serene as a church, entirely in-keeping with its status as an Edinburgh institution. Wood-panelled display cabinets, a deep green carpet, and chandeliers hanging from the ceiling were a throwback to a bygone age. The staff matched the stiff and austere surroundings, walking around the place as if on castors with nary a sound except the creak of rigorously polished shoe leather.

"Good afternoon sir, how may I assist you today?"

Brian found himself face to face with Basil Rathbone's doppleganger.

"Yes, good afternoon. I'd like to see that Rolex Daytona you have in the window please. It's the stainless steel one with the champagne face."

"Certainly. If you'd care to take a seat, I'll bring it right out."

The sales clerk did a one-eighty degree and creaked across the carpet to a wood-panelled door, which he proceeded to open and disappear through. Brian passed the time looking at the contents of the row of display cases arrayed against the wall in front of him, filled with jewellery of every kind, shimmering like the secrets to eternal happiness. Brian next became conscious of the presence of the other sales clerks, standing close together with their hands crossed in front of them, waiting for customers. They could do little else as there wasn't a spec of dust anywhere to be seen; everything was spotless with not a chair out of place.

"Nice day today," Brian said finally, cracking under the tension of the awkward silence.

A small woman, attired in a black skirt-suit, replied, "Yes, isn't it?"

Brian smiled, began tapping his fingers on top of the desk in front of him, pursed his lips and started whistling.

"How's business been?" he said, again unable to stand the silence. The same woman replied. "Quite busy." "I'm not surprised," Brian said. "You carry some beautiful pieces." "Thank you," she said, "I'm glad you like them."

Brian looked away from the woman, who at least was trying to engage with him, and turned his attention to the tall skinny chap, looking on with what Brian took to be a disapproving air. He wouldn't have been out of place asthe butler to some eighteenth-century aristocrat, such was his bearing and distinct air of disdain for those he deemed unworthy.

"Is everything all right?" Brian asked him, the words leaving his mouth on the back of an unexpected surge of irritation.

"I beg your pardon?"

"I only ask because you don't look quite right. I'm a doctor. I know these things."

The man's expression changed and he beat a hasty retreat, walking through the same door his colleague passed through just minutes before. Brian watched him leave then reverted his attention to the display cases in front of him, sure he could detect the glimmer of a smirk from the female member of staff he'd spoken to originally as his gaze passed over her.

Another round of finger tapping and whistling ensued. More time passed, until finally Brian got up from the chair, walked over to the door and left, exchanging a nod with the doorman on the way out. When Brian left Harvey Nichols with Tania, Callum, Gerry and Gareth spent the next half hour at the table trying to come to terms with their friend's good fortune. In the process it was all "What a lucky this and a lucky that."

Gareth and Callum were genuinely happy for him — at least, so they made out. Truth be told, they were both sick with envy but unwilling to admit it. As for Gerry, after being humiliated yet again over the two girls at the table who'd given him the bum's rush by arranging to meet him later at a wine bar that had gone out of business and was no more, he decided to head back to the gym for another workout.

"Are you sure that's the answer?" Gareth chided him when he announced his intention and was about to take off.

"Don't take it personally," Callum chimed in. "Happens to us all."

"Speak for yourself," Gareth said.

"I'll see you tonight," Gerry told them. "What is the plan for tonight anyway?"

"Got a table booked at Andaluz for eight," Callum informed him. "After that just the usual, I think,"

"Okay, later then," Gerry said, before taking his leave and walking through the restaurant to the elevators a despondent and disappointed man. Pierre bade him farewell on his way out, but such was his state of mind Gerry Scott was unable to muster up the effort to respond with even a cursory goodbye.

In the lift on the way down to the exit all he could think about was how where women were concerned he was a dud. I just don't fucking get it, he thought, running it over in his mind. I really don't. He lingered outside the lift on the ground floor to study his reflection in the mirrored wall adjacent to the exit. Look at me. I'm tall (Gerry stood 5'9" in his stocking soles), lean with good skin tone. My hair's still happening too (paying 80 quid for a hair cut at a top salon every other week, so it should be). As for my wardrobe, it couldn't be better.

So what on earth's the problem?

He left Harvey Nichols and walked in the direction of the St James Centre. He'd left his car at the Omni Centre and decided to walk there via John Lewis, affording him the opportunity to have a look at the rugs located on the lower ground floor, thinking he might invest in one for his flat. Along Multrees Walk he went, passing the fashion stores and cafes arrayed on either side. He scanned the tables outside Crolla's coffee shop and restaurant to his left, looking to see if he knew any faces among the people sitting outside drinking lattes and cappuccinos, walking past while conscious of his gait in anticipation of admiring looks coming his way.

Approaching the back entrance to the St James Centre a discernible change in demographic became apparent. Here, Gerry found himself back among the underclass he dealt with every day at work. The place was home to a plethora of shops and outlets configured to meet the needs of the lower end of the retail market, and as soon as you entered the place you were pulled down by an oppressive atmosphere. Like an oasis in a desert John Lewis was located here, but apart from that the St James Centre came squarely into the category of a place to be avoided. Normally, when visiting John Lewis, Gerry would access it through the Leith Street entrance on the other side of the centre. He was quickly reminded why as he walked at pace through the centre now, forced to navigate countless baseball cap wearing neds, many of them in the company of partners with dyed hair, chewing gum, pushing buggies in front of them in which their brats were invariably crying and screaming.

And then up it rose, a voice coming from somewhere behind him.

"Yo…Kamikaze!"

Gerry immediate response was to put his head down up his pace as he rounded the corner and sighted John Lewis at the other end of the crowded concourse, its entrance suddenly assuming the significance of a sanctuary amid a swamp of misery, vulgarity and lowlife.

"Kamikaze," the voice rang out again. It was followed by a whistle, renting the very air, prompting Gerry to up his pace still further, drawing attention to himself but at this point past caring, eyes focused like laser beams on his objective. Such was his determination and desperation to reach John Lewis, he didn't even stop to watch two store security guards attempt to apprehend two suspected shoplifters and the resulting fight when the latter began throwing punches. Gerry instead continued on through the store, hitting the cosmetics section located adjacent to the entrance, passing the girls behind the various counters with the pungent aroma of fragrances sticking in his throat and making his eyes water. In addition to checking out rugs, he was after a jump-drive for his computer, and with this in mind stepped onto the down escalator to the basement and the store's vast electrical and electronics department.

The computing section was busy, but Gerry knew what he was looking for and quickly managed to locate the shelves where the accessories were displayed. They carried a range of jumpdrives of various makes and size and Gerry zeroed in on the most expensive, an 8GB one priced at 160-quid.

He picked it off the peg and turned to the cash desk. The line was ridiculously long (John Lewis, Gerry had always felt, was notoriously understaffed), and instead of waiting he decided to meander through the store to another department in the hope of finding a cash desk less busy. It was just as he set off that his eyes landed on the tall blonde a few feet ahead of him, experiencing a rush of blood to the face as soon as he did. Oblivious to the attention she'd just attracted from the guy behind her, on she walked, meandering through the place in the direction of the escalators at the other end of the store. On impulse, Gerry decided to follow her. *She's so beautiful*, he thought to himself. *I have to try and get her attention.*

The tall blonde went through the revolving door, turned left and began walking in the direction of York Place. Following, Gerry upped his pace in an effort to close the distance. His intention was to get her attention before she reached the pedestrian crossing, which would be too busy with people to make any approach wise.

Suddenly, she stopped walking and turned round to face him.

"Excuse me," she addressed Gerry beneath a furrowed brow, "are you following me by any chance?"

"Eh…sorry?"

"I'll get the police," she went on, regarding Gerry now with a brand of distaste associated with fecal matter.

"No…well….I wasn't following you, but now that you mention it would…I mean…" He coughed. "Look, I was wondering if…."

"You're nothing but a sad little man," she said, interrupting him. "Please go away."

Gerry stood watching as she headed off again, brain doing somersaults as it processed the exchange that had just taken place. Pride, self respect, dignity, the very words now taunting him as the tall blonde's rejection sliced his insides like a cutlass. Seconds passed before he became aware of the fact that he had something in his right hand. The jumpdrive; unwittingly, he'd left the store without paying for it.

Gerry looked back in the direction of John Lewis, vaguely expecting a couple of security guards to be heading his way. They weren't. Nobody was. And in that instant the knowledge he'd left with a 160-quid piece of merchandise in his hand produced a surge of adrenalin that left him near giddy, banishing completely the humiliation of the tall blonde's rejection.

What tall blonde? What rejection?

I'm a man that walks out of department stores with 160-quid jumpdrives in his hand without even as much as a second's thought. Continuing along the street with this in mind, rather than crushed Gerry Scott felt something close to invincible.

## 7

*...but to love foolishly is better than not to be able to love at all*

Gareth, Callum and Gerry were at the gym putting themselves through another arms and shoulders workout in the free weights area. This evening's session began with a superset of dumbbell shoulder presses and side lateral raises; the former designed to develop the entire shoulder muscle, the latter to isolate and emphasise development of the side deltoid to accentuate that all-important illusion of shoulder width.

Of the three, Callum was the most serious when it came to training shoulders; his delts were lagging behind, he did not deny it, and required extra work. Naturally narrow shouldered, he was determined to remedy this genetic deficiency and so took his place on the bench to begin his next superset with his adrenalin pumping. Gerry had just managed eight reps with 40lb dumbbells on shoulder press, before going on to complete ten reps of lat raises with a pair of 10s. He was strong today and Callum was determined to best him. After taking the requisite few seconds to psyche himself up, staring at his reflection in the mirror as he focused in on the set — on the pain he was about to endure in the cause of physical perfection — Callum leaned over, wrapped a hand round the handle of each of the 40lb dumbbells lying on the floor by his feet, and with a one and a two used the momentum of sitting back upright to heave the weights up off the floor onto the top of his shoulders.

He next pushed the dumbbells up off his shoulders until they met at the top of the pressing movement with a clang. From there he lowered the weights to the top of his shoulders again in a controlled fashion, before pushing them back up to complete another rep. By the time he'd completed seven such reps he was struggling, his face red and his arms shaking with effort.

In the background, Gerry voiced words of encouragement. "Come on Callum, keep going pal. You can do this."

Even as these words of encouragement were leaving his mouth, inside he Gerry aglow with the knowledge that Callum wasn't going to match the ten reps he just managed on the same exercise. Sure enough, after completing eight, Callum's arms gave way and he was forced to abandon the set and put the dumbbells down again, using his last ounce of strength to make sure he did so in a controlled manner and didn't drop them on the floor with an ignominious clatter and thereby attract the wrong kind of attention.

Gerry walked forward and gave him a patronising pat on the back as he stood up off the bench. "Well done mate. Your strength's definitely improved."

Callum still had the second half of his superset to complete and with this in mind he got up from the bench, bent over and picked up the 10lb dumbbells that were also lying at his feet on the floor. His shoulders were on fire with lactic acid from the very first rep and by the fourth he was struggling to raise the dumbbells past shoulder level. Finally, after just five reps — half the number Gerry had managed — he stopped and put the weights down again.

Gerry was so elated, looking on, that he was swinging on an imaginary trapeze. Externally, he remained suitably impassive with his attention fixed on Gareth, whose turn it was next.

Half an hour later, the workout over, they were back in the sauna luxuriating in the afterglow of another endorphin fix. The main topic of conversation this evening was Brian. He was meant to have been at the gym training with them tonight but sent Callum a message earlier, cancelling. He didn't give any specific reason as to why he wasn't going to make it, just said he couldn't and left it at that.

"Don't tell me he's so loved up he's missing the gym now," Gerry said.

"Na, not Brian," Gareth said. "He wouldn't do that." Then, after a short pause, "Would he?"

Callum sighed. "I wouldn't have thought so. But then…"

"But then what?" Gerry said, prompting him.

"The way he completely lost his mind when she walked into the restaurant this afternoon. I've never seen him like that before."

"Yes, you've got a point," came Gareth's reply. "He really did flip out."

"You think he's actually fallen for her then?"

In response to Gerry's question, Gareth and Callum looked at one another with the gravity of two world leaders discussing the possibilities of world peace.

"I don't know," Callum said finally. "It's a possibility."

"Yes," an equally thoughtful Gareth agreed, "it's definitely a possibility.

The topic of conversation, Brian, was at that exact moment sitting in his flat staring at the wall, consumed with thoughts of Tania; this woman he'd met earlier that afternoon and whom he hadn't been able to get off his mind since.

The fact he couldn't stop thinking about her was causing him almost as much pain as the memory of her rejection. For as long as he could remember he'd considered himself inured to a woman's charms. No matter how gorgeous or sexy, no matter how engaging, no woman had been able to get inside his head in the two years he'd been single. This one had, with the fact she'd managed it after just one brief meeting a particular worry. The simple truth is that he was smitten.

Sitting in his living room now, he was experiencing the butterflies in the stomach and beating heart of a man whose emotions were in turmoil. Trying to fight it, indeed he was, and also trying to rationalise his feelings as a natural response to the manner in which she'd rejected him and left him standing outside the hotel like a fool. His pride had been dented, that was all, is what he attempted to convince himself. By this time tomorrow, he'll have put it all behind him and have moved on.

Yet despite his valiant attempt to rationalise it in such terms, it was no use. Brian knew that what he was feeling was down to far more than pride. Something about this woman had left him determined to see her again. What was it? Her looks? Yes, she was absolutely ravishing. But even so, looks alone weren't enough to cause him to be so utterly fixated on her to this extent.

Shit, she's inside my head, he thought glumly, staring at the wall with the only sound the lugubrious ticking of antique grandfather clock in the corner of the room. And as much as he resisted an increasingly powerful urge to return to the hotel to try and see her again, it was impossible. He *had* to see her again and *was* going to see her again — tonight.

Half an hour later a cab pulled up outside The Balmoral Hotel. It was a balmy night, the sky was absent of cloud, and after paying the driver Brian got out while struggling to maintain his balance due to the mammoth bunch of flowers he had in his left hand. As soon as he hit the pavement dozens of pairs of eyes immediately fastened on him. From the bus stop twenty feet along the street to his right arrived wolf whistles from a group of young lads, while passengers on passing buses smiled at the sight of him heading up the steps to the entrance of the hotel with a big bunch of flowers in his hand.

Fred the doorman hit him with a knowing smile as he opened the door for him on the way in. In his fifteen years in the job he'd seen just about everything it was possible to see — from the positively ridiculous to the equally sublime — leaving him decidedly unimpressed by any of it. Still, he never tired of enjoying watching people making fools of themselves, especially the kind of people who could afford to stay at one of Scotland's most salubrious hotels.

Though conscious of the attention he was receiving, Brian was too determined and focused to be in any way put off from carrying out his mission and made great haste in walking from the cab up the steps and on into the relative sanctuary of the hotel.

Once inside, he paused for a few moments to collect himself. He'd spent an hour agonising over what to wear, trying on three or four different ensembles until settling on his navy linen suit by Armani. He purchased the suit this time last year at Harrods in London and tonight decided to complement it with a crisp white shirt by Nicole Fahri and on his feet a pair of light brown canvas shoes by Hugo Boss. Dangling from his left wrist was his Breitling with the brown leather strap. Over the past few weeks he'd gone off the stainless steel bracelet watches he normally wore, deciding that they erred on the wrong side of ostentation.

Having collected himself, it was time to continue with his objective. With this in mind, Brian began walking confidently across the hotel foyer's plush carpet in the direction of reception, relieved to see there was nobody there apart from the two members of staff. The anxiety and doubt he'd experienced on the way over melted away as he strode the final few feet to reception like a man who had the world by the gonads.

The two clerks behind the desk comprised one male and one female — the man somewhere in his mid thirties, the girl in her mid to late twenties. Just as Brian made his approach the girl disappeared through a door behind the desk to take her break. This left only the male clerk to deal and as Brian approached the desk he looked up and met with a perfunctory.

"Yes sir, how may I help you?"

"Hi," Brian answered the man, whose name badge revealed was called Michael. "I'm here to deliver these to Tania. She's staying here."

Michael took a second. "Is there a last name?"

"I just know her first name," Brian replied, doing so with the kind of conviction designed to circumvent such trivial details. "She's an American, here visiting from New York."

"Is she expecting you?"

"Yes…no…em, not really. She'll want to see me though."

For a man like Michael, who'd worked in hospitality since leaving school, dealing with nutters was his bread

"I'm sorry," he said matter-of-factly, "we have a strict policy at this hotel. We can't…"

"Please," Brian implored, "you have to help me. She's the one. Do you understand? I mean this is Casablanca when Bogie bumps into Ingrid Bergman in Rick's Cafe. It's Top Gun, when Tom Cruise walks into that bar. It's…."

"Yes," Michael interrupted him, "I get the idea."

But Brian was in full flow now and wouldn't be denied. "Fate is what this is," he continued. "Do you believe in fate, Michael?"

"No."

"Okay, well, remember the last time you fell in love?"

"Hasn't happened to me since the last time I looked in the mirror."

This last remark succeeded in stopping Brian in his tracks, rendering him unable to come up with a suitable rejoinder by which to penetrate the guy standing before him's wall of intransigence. But he was in luck, as the resulting pause and crushing disappointment written on his face had the effect of softening Michael's sense of duty. Against usual practice in such situations he went to his computer and brought up the guest register. After a few seconds, he looked up.

"We have a Tania Gonzalez currently staying with us."

"That's her," Brian said. "It has to be."

"Okay, one moment please," Michael said, before picking up the phone and dialling the room.

"Good evening Miss Gonzalez, this is Michael down at reception. I'm sorry to trouble you, but I have a gentleman here who wishes to see you." Brian looked on with his heart pounding. "Tell her it's Brian, the guy she had lunch with today," he prompted.

"His name is Brian and he says the two of you had lunch today."

There was a pause as Michael listened to Tania on the other end of the line. Finally, after what seemed an interminable period of time, Michael ended the call with, "Certainly madam. I'm so sorry to have bothered you. Have a pleasant evening." Michael placed the phone back down. "She said that she's too busy to see you. You may leave the flowers with me if you wish. I'll see that she gets them."

Without a word, Brian handed the flowers over the counter. He attempted a smile but his disappointment wouldn't allow it and instead he left Michael at the desk with a weak nod. As he trudged back across the plush red carpet towards the hotel's exit he felt a tonne weight bearing down.

All hope was lost and ruefully it came to him — the extent to which he'd fallen for this woman he'd only just met. What the hell's happened to you? Now there could be no hiding or mitigating the blow to his self-esteem, not to mention dignity. Walking past a smiling-saluting Fred at the door, Brian hit the street and continued on walking without looking back.

## 8

*You don't find love, it finds you*

Later that night Gerry, Gareth and Callum were at Tigerlily, occupying their regular booth in the back. For a Saturday night the place was noticeably quiet.

"This place is a morgue tonight," Gareth said, articulating what the three of them were thinking.

"Yep," Callum said, "looks like the shit is really starting to bite with the economy."

"I need to go pee," Gerry said, intruding on the exchange. "Be right back." And so saying he got up and headed for the gents downstairs.

"How are you managing just now?" Gareth asked Callum.

"Still okay," Callum answered confidently. "Edinburgh's property market is more or less recession proof."

They were of course discussing the ongoing recession, which began life as the credit crunch in late 2007 and which by now, in mid-2008, had morphed into a full blown global economic downturn. As yet it had made little impact on the lives and lifestyles of Brian, Callum, Gerry and Gareth, and given that they were committed to maintaining that lifestyle no matter what, such serious topics were normally off limits, especially on a night out. It's why Gerry had left so abruptly for the toilet and why now, as Gareth kept banging on, Callum was growing irritated.

"I wouldn't be so sure," Gareth opined. "Not with the way things are headed. I've had two business deals collapse this month already and it's only the fifteenth."

"Really?"

"Yes, really. At this rate I'll be forced to live on the bare salary of an MSP."

"Oh that's right, I forgot," Callum said, attempting to lighten the tone, "you're Mr Ten Percent."

"Mr Zero Percent right now," Gareth replied laconically.

At that precise moment Gerry returned. "Should we try him again?" he said.

"We've tried calling him three times now," Callum reminded him.

"It's not right," Gareth said. "He's got six nights a week to spend with this woman. Saturday nights are sacred." Gerry produced his phone. "Let me ping him a text."

It was just as Gerry was about to do so that Brian appeared, coming towards them through the bar looking decidedly down in the dumps.

"Speak of the devil," Gerry said when he arrived in their midst. "I was just about to text you."

"So tell us," Callum said. "How'd it go? Did you…?"

"Yes, how was it?" Gareth said with a grin. "Is she as good as she looks?"

Brian had prepared himself for this very moment with the decision to tell them the truth about how badly it all turned out and why, given their role in precipitating it with their stupid antics. Before he could open his mouth, however, Gareth drew everybody's attention over to the other side of the bar, where Tania at that precise moment was standing in the company of some guy.

Stunned silence met the sight. In that moment all questions with regard to Brian's time with Tania had just been answered and instantly they felt sorry for him, standing there reduced to helplessness in the face of his continuing humiliation at the hands of this female. How now he wished he'd never set eyes on her.

Callum was first to speak. "Okay," he said, finishing his drink, "I don't know about everyone else, but I'm up for trying the Living Room for a change tonight."

"Agreed," Gareth said, making a move. "This place is dead tonight."

"Gerry?" Callum said, prompting him with a subtle nod of the head. But Gerry failed to take the hint. "Give it time. It's still early," he said. Gareth and Callum then hit him with a look that went beyond the realms of a subtle hint.

"Then again," Gerry corrected himself, "might be good to try somewhere else for a change?" Finishing his drink he followed behind Gareth, who'd already begun making his way through the bar on his way out.

Before departing, Callum placed a sympathetic hand on Brian's shoulder. "Come on mate" he said. "You look like you could do with a drink."

Brian nodded, was just about to follow him on the way out, when Tania appeared in front of him with the guy she was with. Such was his state of mind, Brian hadn't noticed her approaching from across the other side of the bar.

"Well, isn't this a surprise?" she said, smiling.

Brian was speechless, not to mention embarrassed, while Callum was embarrassed for him.

"This is John," Tania went on, referring to her date. "John, this is Brian."

"Nice to meet you Brian," John said with his hand outstretched.

Brian shook John's had without enthusiasm; he couldn't remember ever feeling this crushed, a feeling only made worse by the fact Tania looked even more beautiful than she had when he first set eyes on her. She had on a tight black dress and had her tied up to reveal more of her face and a neck that was long and as smooth as polished marble. The very sight of her was akin to some heinous medieval torture.

"Listen," Callum said to Brian, butting in, "I'll see you over there when you're ready."

Brian didn't respond and Callum took off, relieved to be making his escape.

"Twice in one day," Tania said. "How funny."

She followed her remark with a sip of her drink through the straw in her glass, all the while looking at him. Was he imagining it? Was she flirting with him? What the hell is she playing at? If she's trying to make a fool of me in front of her date, I'll…I'll…I don't know what I'll do, but I'll do something.

"Funny?" Brian replied. "Yes, well, I suppose you could say that."

"Sorry I wasn't able to see you earlier. I was getting ready to meet John."

At this Brian's cheeks flushed red.

"Is that right?" he said, looking at her, in the process completely ignoring John, who was still hovering in the background.

"Speaking of which," John said as if on cue, "I'd better be off. My other half will be wondering where I've got to." With that he finished his drink and placed his empty glass down on the table adjacent. "Let's go over those details on Monday morning," he said to Tania.

"Okay, sounds good," she said.

John leaned over and kissed her on the cheek before turning his attention to Brian, who by now was completely nonplussed.

"Nice meeting you. Have a good night."

"Yes, cheers…you too," Brian replied as they shook hands for a second time. John then about turned and took off.

"Tania had a smile on her face. She was enjoying the confusion that was all over Brian's as he watched John make his way through the bar, which had grown significantly busier over the past few minutes.

Turning his attention back to Tania, Brian said: "I thought…"

"You thought we were together," Tania said, finishing his sentence for him. "John's a broker with an investment company I'm doing business with over here. We went out to dinner to discuss a business deal. He's married. Happily too, it seems. Not that common nowadays, wouldn't you say?"

"So?" he ventured hopefully.

"Nice flowers."

Brian blushing now. "Thanks, I'm glad you liked them."

Tania finished her drink. "I don't know about you, but I could do with another."

"Wait at minute. How come you ended up here. Did you…"

"You invited me here, remember?

Brian took a moment. "Yes, I did."

"It's rare that a man's willing to go to the trouble of embarrassing himself in public in pursuit of a woman who previously rejected him."

"And so?"

"And so here I am."

Brian looked at her, smiling. "Let's get that drink."

At one in the morning George Street was awash with groups of men and women making their way either from or to one of the various clubs and late night bars strung along its length. Even in July it gets cold in Edinburgh at night, and tonight a strong easterly breeze had the girls in their summer dresses wishing they'd brought a jacket. As for the guys, mostly dressed in shirts or tight fitting t-shirts, they were inured to the temperature by an excess of alcohol and whatever else they'd imbibed. Thus, the only thing on their minds was continuing to have a good time.

Downstairs from Tigerlily in Lulu, Gareth and Callum had already scored and were in different parts of the club getting to know the females in question. Gareth was seated next a dark skinned brunette on the plush couches over against the far wall, while Callum was standing at the bar pressed up close to a tall girl with long chestnut hair who was in Edinburgh from Belfast for the weekend with a group of friends.

This left Gerry the odd man out, though not for long if he had anything to do with it; for at that precise second he was preparing to move in on the two girls standing by one of the pillars just five feet away. A final sip of his drink, a quick hand through the hair, and he was ready.

"Hey girls, how's it going? I'm Gerry."

"Fuck off."

"Sorry?"

The girl who'd just spoken for the two of them was called Sandra. From Drylaw, she was as rough as a badger's arse.

"Ye deef?" she said, glaring at him. "Beat it."

Though the venom in her voice placed Gerry on the back foot, he could not conceive of beating a retreat, and so determined to press on regardless, he came back, "So how's your night been? Having a good one?" This time the girls ignored him completely. "I'm minted by the way," Gerry continued regardless. "Want a drink?"

The other girl turned to him this time. "We're fine," she said. "If ye dinnae mind, we're huvin' a private conversation."

"You're fine? Okay."

The girls returned to their conversation, leaving Gerry standing there feeling stupid and looking even stupider. It got even worse when he happened to look round and noticed Callum with his tongue down the throat of the girl from Belfast at the bar. Like a hand grenade going off inside his brain, Gerry reacted by grabbing Sandra from Drylaw, pulling her to him and kissing her on the lips.

The second he did chaos erupted; Sandra struggling and thrashing her arms around in the air like a mad woman as she tried to break free; her friend Donna mounting a vicious attack at the same time, scratching and punching Gerry with righteous ferocity. No matter, Gerry was determined to hang on. She'll come round! She'll come round! This was the thought that kept repeating inside his by now very confused not to mention disturbed mind. It was now that Big Jimmy appeared and pulled Gerry away from his girlfriend with a massive shovel-like hand.

"Woe ya cunt, she's wi' me!"

"I'm sorry! I didn't know! I..!"

Big Jimmy's fist connected with Gerry's nose and the instant he did a curtain of white stars descended inside his brain just as the bouncers arrived on the scene to clean up the mess.

## 9

*We are all mortal until the first kiss, and second glass of wine*

As Gerry was being scooped up off the floor at Lulu nightclub and carted out by the bouncers, Brian and Tania were walking through Edinburgh's New Town hand in hand. For the past couple of hours, back at Tigerlily, they'd been so engrossed in one another that nothing and no one else had mattered, even existed. Now they were walking in the direction of Brian's flat on Abercromby Place. It was a beautiful night, despite the cool breeze, and as they walked Tania was spellbound by the history and architecture that predominated.

"This really is a beautiful city," she said. "Cold but beautiful. You're so lucky this is home."

Brian stopped walking and removed his jacket. "Here," he said, placing it over her shoulders. He then took her hand again and they continued walking.

"You know what, I actually think…"

"Think what?"

She giggled. "Na, it's okay. I was going to say something, but I won't as the wine's gone to my head and I might make a fool of myself.

"Kinda like you with the flowers."

"What a cheek," Brian replied, laughing.

They walked on, enjoying the relative tranquility down here away from George Street late on a Saturday night. Brian was glowing inside. Never had he felt so attracted to a woman before. It was as if a door had appeared in front of him, beckoning him to walk through into a world of happiness he never knew existed.

They fucked all night, only stopping to rest and drink some water periodically. In the morning they fucked again then went for breakfast at Hector's in Stockbridge. When Tania told him over her scrambled eggs and avocado that the sex was the best she'd ever had, Brian didn't know what to say.

Thereafter, they spent every spare moment together. They went to Princes Street Gardens, where between cavorting on the grass and eating ice cream like two lovestruck teenagers, they talked about their respective lives, love and loss. As the days passed, Brian found himself changing in ways that took him by surprise. Thoughts of going to the gym, of shopping at Harvey Nichols — of his status and reputation as a man about town — paled when compared to how he felt in Tania's company. All he desired now was to be with her, feel her hand in his, smell her hair, to see her smile and hear her laugh.

They spent one afternoon on an open-top tour bus taking in the sights, something that Brian would normally never consider doing with anyone apart from his kids. Tania was in her element viewing Edinburgh's abundant monuments, historic buildings and landmarks, cooing as she pointed here, there and elsewhere from the top of the tour bus.

It was at Brian's insistence that they devoted an entire afternoon to visiting Edinburgh Castle, exploring its museums, ramparts, and various statues and monuments to Scotland's ancient kings and queens, digesting Scotland's long and dramatic history. They stood on the ramparts with their arms wrapped around one another, looking out at the panoramic view of Princes Street, the New Town, and the River Forth shining and shimmering like a jewel beyond, its world-famous road and rail bridges crossing its breadth like two giant red ribbons.

They went for lunch, over which they talked and laughed like two people hopelessly infatuated; the speed with which it was happening rendering them both stunned. Discussing it, Brian revealed that it was the way she had shown him up outside the hotel on the first day they met that piqued his interest, producing feelings that went beyond his usual desire for sexual conquest and gratification.

As for Tania, it was the vulnerability Brian had demonstrated by returning to the hotel with flowers that did the trick. It proved to her she'd been wrong in her initial impression of him as nothing more than a player with an ego the size of a mountain. This change of opinion, she went on to explain, was confirmed by his reaction when she arrived at Tigerlily and saw how crestfallen he looked when he first saw her with John, her business associate. As for her appearance at Tigerlily, this was no accident; she remembered Brian inviting her there outside the hotel and had turned up hoping to see him.

It was the kind of exchange that causes the insides to tingle, and from that moment they both knew they were in the midst of something that had the potential to be special. This was only confirmed when they were in bed together.

Throughout this period the guys were constantly calling and texting Brian in an effort to find out what was going on; why he'd suddenly stopped going to the gym or meeting up at Harvey Nicks for shopping and plan their next foray into Edinburgh's nightlife? It was as if he'd just disappeared, which in a certain sense he had. Because without planning to or being conscious of it, Brian Davison had now jettisoned his old life.

What did it matter if he went to the gym or ate ice cream and indulged himself? Who cared if he was wearing the latest Prada or Armani? And as far as going out, he still wanted to but with this woman instead of them — and not to Tigerlily or any of the other old haunts in George Street, but now to the theatre or cinema and thereafter a quiet restaurant for a bite to eat.

The more time he spent with Tania the more Brian realised how empty and devoid of meaning these past two years. Since his divorce from Gail he'd convinced himself he didn't need anyone special, believing that all he needed to be happy was to have fun, splash out on designer clothes and other luxuries, and bed different women without getting attached to them. Intimacy, companionship, devotion, love; mere words that turned grown adults into babbling wrecks, he decided, words that people embrace in a futile attempt to fill a void. Weak, insecure people needed relationships; strong, independent people — people like him — did not.

But after meeting and falling for Tania, he was forced to admit that such a cynical analysis of relationships and commitment had been wrong. In denying himself the kind of happiness that can only be found in a relationship, Brian developed a cold, harsh outlook when it came to life, and had consequently lost out.

A qualitative change came over him. This manifested most significantly in his attitude towards his duties as a GP. Previously, he'd barely been able to conceal the contempt in which he held his patients. In they would come, one after the other, suffering with health issues connected to the consumption of copious quantities of bad food, cigarettes and alcohol, combined with a lack of exercise. They were people from that sector of society social commentators described as the underclass — people with low self-esteem and little if any prospects of being anything other than a drain on the NHS. This was how Brian viewed them previously.

Now he began to rediscover compassion and sympathy for those less fortunate that he hadn't experienced in years.

Where before he blamed them for their lack of education, manners and poverty, now he began to see them as victims of circumstances beyond their control. In essence he was no longer blind to the fact their plight was the result of grievous inequality, which only increased year on year.

Instead, he had been was reunited with those idealistic principles he'd owned back when he was a medical student and had visions of making a difference, helping to bring succour to people whose lives were reduced to a daily struggle for survival in the developing world.

Those lofty principles began to be eroded when he first started work as a GP in Edinburgh for the NHS and encountered what passed for poverty in his native land for the first time. With his background ensuring that he'd been more or less cocooned from society's rougher areas and elements while growing up, combined with his experience of spending a year in Africa as a medical student, he'd found it impossible to feel any compassion for people who came into his surgery trying to wangle sick notes they weren't entitled to and free prescriptions to help treat self-inflicted illnesses and conditions.

He now saw those same people through different eyes. They were the product of a harsh environment which in turn had made them harsh. No wonder they ate crap, smoked and drank to excess, he came round to thinking. So would I, so would anyone in their situation.

No doubt about it, he was a changed man. And to think those changes had come after just a few short weeks in the company of a woman who'd arrived in his life completely out of nowhere. It was just as Oscar Wilde said: 'Every sinner has a future, and every saint has a past.'

A couple of nights later, Gareth and Callum were at the gym in the middle of a tough spinning class. Spinning was something they did every now and then as a change from the treadmill, their preferred mode of cardio.

The best thing about a spinning class was that there were always a few babes to look at, which helped take your mind off the pain. This evening there were more than the usual complement in attendance, and in response the guys were giving it their all in an effort to impress.

It must have worked because as soon as the session came to an end, the petite redhead on the bike next to Gareth's flashed him a coquettish smile as she wiped the sweat from her face with a towel. Gareth smiled back, whereupon she engaged him in conversation.

"You don't recognise me, do you?" she said.

"Eh, no…sorry, I don't think I do," he answered. "Should I?"

"You dated my sister for a short while at the beginning of last year."

"Did I?"

"Yes, you did. Her name's Jackie."

"Oh, Jackie," Gareth said, feigning recognition. "How is she?"

The petite redhead climbed off her bike. "She's great. She's married and lives in London now."

Gareth climbed off his bike whilst continuing to wipe himself down. Callum had already left the studio to go and lift some weights.

"Well," Gareth said, "good for her. It's good to hear she's well."

The girl smiled and started for the door.

"Look," Gareth said, catching up to her, "it'd be nice to keep in touch. Maybe we could go for a drink sometime."

They exited the studio and stopped to continue their exchange. "Eh, yeah, that would be cool," she said.

"Great," Gareth said, face lighting up.

"I'll bring my fiancé," she told him.

Twenty minutes later, the workout over, Gareth and Callum were relaxing in the sauna. The topic of conversation was Gerry and last weekend's incident at Lulus, when he'd ended up on the wrong end of a fist after trying to force himself on someone else's girlfriend.

"I've tried calling him three or four times in the last couple of days," Gareth was saying, "but he isn't picking up."

"Maybe we should go round and make sure he's okay. He's obviously humiliated."

"So he should be, behaving like that. What the hell was he thinking?"

"I still say we should check on him."

"Personally, I'm more worried about Brian," Gareth said, bored talking about Gerry and eager to change the subject.

"You may have a point there, actually."

"The way he's going on with this woman…it's sad. Have you seen him lately? He's like love's young dream."

"Hasn't been to the gym in over two weeks," Callum added. "Plus he's missed the last three Saturday nights out.

"Maybe he's ill?"

"It wouldn't surprise me if he announced that he's asked her to marry him."

"I really think he might be ill," Callum said again.

There was a pause as they both considered the situation. "Anyway, it's time for my facial," Callum said next as he got up off the bench and threw his towel around his waist

"What happened to going round to check on Gerry?"

"I will," Callum answered, pushing open the door and stepping out. "Just as soon as I've had my facial."

"Fair shout," Gareth said as he got up and followed him out. "A man has to get his priorities right."

Half an hour later they were luxuriating in the spa, sitting side by side having their regular facial. Their faces were coated in oil and patches covered their eyes. The aestheticians treating them had left the room to allow their skin to absorb the oil for ten minutes.

"So I'm undecided whether to get the new Range Rover Sport or another X5," Gareth was saying, continuing the thread of the conversation they were having. "What do you think?"

"In this month's Arena there's an interesting article on hybrids. They seem to be very much in vogue right now. Tom Cruise is driving one."

"Is he really?" Gareth replied. "He also flies around the world in a private jet. I wonder how that's going down with Greenpeace?"

"All I'm saying is that hybrids are better for the environment and that the environment is on trend these days."

"I'll stick to a good old fashioned petrol of diesel motor, thank you very much."

"You're an MSP. You're meant to set an example."

"No, Callum," Gareth replied. "I'm a man of impeccable taste who happens to be an MSP."

Callum said nothing in response to that.

"So what do you think? The new Range Rover Sport or an X5?"

"Range Rover," Callum said.

"Yes, that's what I was thinking."

"And maybe a hybrid as a Sunday car. Just to ease the conscience a little."

"You drive one if you want to," Gareth replied dismissively. "Personally, I'd rather stick my head up an elephant's arse."

By the time Gareth and Callum left the gym rain was lashing down. It was one of those horribly heavy summer rains that combines with the heat to leave those caught in it drenched and sweating at the same time. The rain and the heat didn't bother either of them, however, as they were comfortably ensconced in top of the range vehicles replete with advanced air con systems.

On their way down to the Shore in Leith to check in on Gerry, they took a diversion away from Leith Walk onto Bonnington Road. On the drive down Gareth was listening to the Black Eyed Peas, while Callum preferred Classic FM on this quiet Sunday afternoon.

Gerry Scott lived in a large three-bedroom flat on the top floor of a newly refurbished tenement block with a spectacular view out over the harbour. At one time the Shore in Leith had been home to prostitutes, dive bars and run down housing.

It was not then a place where you wanted to be out walking alone during the day, much less at night. However the Shore had long since been gentrified and was now home to some of the city's trendier bars, restaurants, hotels and luxury flats. Gerry moved down here after splitting up with his ex four years ago and liked it so much he couldn't see himself living anywhere else again.

At that moment, his door buzzer going in the background, Gerry's mind was on more important matters things than where he lived. With his face still showing the evidence of his physical confrontation at Lulu in the shape of the faded remnants of a black eye, he was on his computer trawling through page after page of women on the dating site he'd just signed up to. Hardly a spare moment had he spent away from his computer since, sending winks to women located far, wide and in-between.

He was gratified to see that many of them had winked back, and now he was busy firing off messages to the ones he liked the look of most. As for the door buzzer, continuing to sound in the background, Gerry knew that it could only be Callum or Gareth — or both — arrived to check up on him. Since the incident in the club he hadn't been able to face them and had ignored their calls and messages.

Today was no different and, anyhow, he'd be damned if he was going to be distracted from the urgent task of finding a woman to date and be seen with. The negative turnaround in his fortunes in this regard was something he couldn't fathom, especially as this time last year it seemed he could do no wrong when it came to women, bedding a different one almost every week.

So what the hell's going on? What's gone wrong?

His appearance hadn't changed; on the contrary, if anything, he was leaner and tighter than last year. Further still, he still dressed well and his skin was in good nick. So what then? Why is it that where women were concerned he was now about as popular as nuclear waste?

Right, he thought, hunched over his computer studying the profile of another prospect, whom judging by her pictures was an attractive brunette in her mid-30s Let's see, first things first: body type. Hmmm, athletic and toned she says. Good. Now, height? Five-nine. Not bad. She doesn't have any kids either and, let's have a quick scroll down, she's an architect. Right, now let's take a look at what she's written.

It was all the usual guff about looking for a man with a sense of humour and adventure; someone who's sensitive and family oriented — a professional, educated man; someone ready to let love into his life.

Fuck, me how wet is that, Gerry thought after reading it. Regardless, this one, he decided, warranted a message. After taking a minute to think, he came up with the following:

> Hi, I just came across you on here and thought I'd venture a message. My name is Gerry and I hope you like my pictures. I've been on a diet and my body fat is currently down at 11%. Cheers, Gerry x

## 10

*Love is the child of illusion, and the parent of disillusion*

July turned to August and for the past three weeks Brian and Tania had been spending every spare moment in each other's company.

Originally only meant to be in Edinburgh ten days, Tania decided to extend her stay with the excuse to her boss in

New York that she'd set up additional meetings to chase up a new leads. Rather than focused on the bank's pressing need to claw back some of the billions it had lost as a result of the financial collapse, as she was meant to be doing, Tania's head was elsewhere. For the first time in a long time the opportunity had presented itself for the kind of happiness she'd almost come round to accepting would never again be hers. Sunday morning and the two of them were in bed at Brian's, having just fucked for the umpteenth time since late last night.

"So, my Scottish man," Tania said, "tell me about you."

"Me?"

"Yep, I want to know everything."

He smiled while placing his hand behind his head on the pillow. "Okay, well, for starters I'm a handsome devil."

"No honey," Tania admonished him, "I'm serious. I want to know what's inside. In your heart."

Brian looked at her. "Wow, you *are* serious."

"Come on baby, work with me here."

"Right, so what do you want to know? Ask away."

Tania snuggled up, resting her hands and head on top of his chest.

"What makes you happy?"

"Hmmm, what makes me happy?" He paused for a moment to think. "Feeling the wind in my face, laughter, a blue sky, shopping…"

"Shopping?" she cut in. "Men aren't supposed to like shopping."

"You happen to be in the company of one who does."

Tania started giggling.

"Oh, so it's funny is it?" he said, smiling at the sight of her laughing. "Let me tell you something…men are no longer living in the dark ages. Nowadays we're in touch with our feminine side."

"You're in touch with your bi side, it sounds to me."

Brian started tickling her.

"Baby, no!" she screamed, laughing and wriggling and squirming in an effort to get away from him. "Stop it!"

He stopped and she settled down again.

"All right smart ass," he quipped, "your turn."

"Okay," she said, "shoot."

"What makes you happy?"

"Let's see now. Feeling the wind in my face, laughter, a blue sky…" Brian started tickling her again. "I'm sorry,

I'm sorry!" she pleaded, again wriggling and squirming in a desperate attempt to escape his grasp.

"I'm bored with this game," Brian said. "Let's fuck again instead." And with that, he began kissing and nibbling at her neck and rubbing her thigh with his hand.

"No, wait," Tania protested. "We can do that later. Baby…wait." Brian stopped as instructed. "Come on now, pay attention," she went on. "Ask me another question and I'll ask you one."

Brian threw his head back on his pillow again with a sigh. "All right, if we must. "Em…ever been married?"

"Yes," Tania said, drawing out the word.

"You had to think about that one."

"Next question," she told him.

"Kids?"

The question hit home and Tania's immediate response was to look away.

"What's wrong?" Brian said, suddenly concerned. "Are you okay?"

"I'm sorry. I'm all right."

"No, something's wrong. You're upset."

Tania wanted to tell him, she really did, but the words refused to come.

"It's..." she began falteringly. "I had a baby. It..." She couldn't bring herself to say the rest and retreated. "It's all right," she continued, fighting back tears. "Just give me a second."

"Are you sure?"

"Yes, I'm fine." Then: "I'm sorry, I feel so stupid."

"No, it's my fault," Brian said, holding her. "I'm sorry, I had no idea this was something..."

"Anyway," Tania said, cutting in before he could finish. "What about you? Do you have children?"

Brian looked at her, absorbed the pain emanating from her eyes, and shook his head.

"Let's change the subject," he suggested. "What's your favourite food?"

"Okay, you first."

"Hmmm, actually that's a hard one." Pausing first to think, Brian said: "A mince pie supper."

"What the hell is that?" she said, screwing up her face and Brian relieved and happy to see the pain gone from her eyes.

"Trust me, you wouldn't understand."

"Okay," she continued, "favourite city."

Brian took a second to think. "New York."

"Music?"

"Eh…Hip-Hop?"

"No, bagpipes," she corrected him.

"Bagpipes?"

"Whenever I hear the sound of bagpipes from now I'm going to think of you. I want you to do the same with me." Brian looked at her. As he did he ran his hand through her hair. Every bit as much as she'd fallen for him, he'd fallen for her. More even. And as if to confirm it, he pulled her to him.

By now the recession was really taking its toll. Reports of countless small and medium size businesses going to the wall, of declining property prices, declining pound, rising unemployment, investment falling and share prices in free fall dominated an increasingly doom-laden news cycle, producing a palpable sense of fear percolating through the streets and filling workplaces.

Offices that were once hives of activity were now sad desultory places where people spent their days trying to look busy in order to justify a salary that now seemed incongruous, even after a ten percent pay cut. Phones that once never stopped ringing rang no more, while empty desks and chairs bore evidence of the mounting casualties of an economy that seemed to have turned in on itself like a collapsing building.

And just like a tidal wave gathering size as it moves perilously close to the shore, the so-called real economy — the one that dealt in things rather than smoke and mirrors — was now also being battered.

Due to the banks placing a squeeze on lending, hardly anyone was buying or selling property, which meant that nobody was building them, with the result that an army of builders, contractors, plumbers, carpenters, scaffolders and others were left with no work.

The banks, formerly considered bastions of financial and moral rectitude and probity, had been uncovered as mass casinos in all but name and flashing neon. They'd been bailed out yet still they refused to lend, still doggedly refusing to underwrite the contracts which to small and medium size businesses were as important as food to the sustenance of life.

Many who were yet to feel the impact, those whose feet were further from the shore and still dry, attempted to ignore the evidence of impending doom and continue as before, harking back to when life was good and an unlimited supply of credit allowed them to purchase anything they desired anytime they wished.

Designer this, that and the other was still fundamental to lives dedicated to self-gratification, hedonism and luxury. Life without shopping, nights out, good wine and food remained impossible to contemplate, even for a second. However, despite the refusal to acknowledge the reality of what was taking place around them, the truth refused to be denied. Slowly and ineluctably, the party was coming to an

At just after four in the afternoon, Gerry Scott left Edinburgh Sheriff Court on Chambers Street, deciding that instead of heading back to the office, he was going to take the rest of the day off. After defending assorted lowlifes all day, he deserved some time to himself. And on a beautiful summer's day like this, what better way to spend those hours than a leisurely hour or two spent browsing the shops, before heading home to get ready for his a date later this evening with the girl he'd just met online? It was the first date he'd arranged since subscribing and he was suitably excited at the prospect.

On then he went, brown Prada calfskin briefcase swinging from his right hand as he strolled along George IV Bridge with its cafes and bars filled mostly by students from the main Edinburgh University campus at Bristo Square.

Contradicting this otherwise rustic picture was the odd group of underclass neds, either on their way to or from the court. They instantly stood out with their pallid and undernourished features, set in an aggressive countenance and topped off by a gait that brought to mind man's Neanderthal origins.

Regardless, the Old Town was a fine part of the city to be out walking in, endowed as it was with such a rich bounty of culture and history, reflected in the opulent buildings, monuments, cathedrals and various other landmarks that abounded here. There had been a time, albeit a few good years ago now, when Gerry harboured an interest in history and historical events to the point of amassing a substantial book collection on the subject. In the intervening years though his interest waned, the books sat on his bookshelf gathering dust, until Gerry gave them away to charity.

Other priorities, such as the gym and ensuring he was never less than sartorially perfect on a given day, took precedence.

Today was no different, dressed as he was in a black Paul Smith suit, Paul Smith light grey shirt, dark grey silk tie by Ferragamo, and on his feet a pair of black handmade pair of Tricker's brogues. His hair was trimmed and styled in accordance with the fashion of the day, and on his face were the Armani sunglasses he'd put on as soon as he left court. Like this he continued on his way, ambling along the street like a man who was well on top.

Crossing a High Street that was choc-a-bloc with tourists, he walked down the Mound and round past the spectacular Bank of Scotland building, continuing on until he emerged from between the buildings on either side to a heart stopping view of Princes Street, Princes Street Gardens, and in the foreground two magnificent examples of nineteenth-century neo-classical Georgian architecture that were home to two of Scotland's oldest and most prestigious art galleries.

As he began descending the steep steps down to Mound Square, the idea of spending an hour partaking art instead of the shops entered his head. By the time he reached the bottom of the steps he'd dismissed the idea. So focused was he on the shops that now lay in the near distance, he failed to notice the young guy sitting on the pavement with his back to the wall begging for change.

On his way across Mound Square, with the hustle and bustle of Princes Street now directly ahead, on Gerry's mind was this evening's workout. He'd been dieting hard these past few weeks, determined to get so lean and ripped there could be no question about who was in better shape between him and Gareth.

Yes, it had been hard eating nothing but salad, rice and lean chicken in ever decreasing quantities for the past month or so, but the results were worth the sacrifice. As for the light headedness that came over him at regular intervals throughout the day due to the lack of glycogen in his system, he'd learned to embrace the feeling as tangible evidence of progress in his quest for physical perfection.

Gerry crossed over to Princes Street and turned right. Normally he and the guys went out of their way to avoid

Princes Street. One of the most famous thoroughfares in Europe, now look at it — a repository of cheap dowdy retail stores, its pavement permanently covered in litter and packed with the kind of people who made the argument in favour of eugenics a compelling one.

But today Gerry was breaking with his regular habit of heading straight up to George Street, where the air seemed cleaner, the shops were better and more exclusive, and the people more fashionably dressed. Today, though, he had business on Princes Street in the shape of a visit to M&S.

Usually, the only thing he every purchased here was food. And whenever he did go food shopping at M&S, it was always at one of the branches located outwith the city centre in one of the various shopping malls located beyond. Today, though, was different — today there was good reason for Gerry to visit the M&S branch on Princes Street. For on this day he was intent on again experiencing the buzz he'd felt when he walked out of John Lewis the other week with a jumpdrive in his hand he hadn't paid for.

Today, Gerry Scott was going shoplifting.

*A little stealing is a dangerous part, but stealing largely is a noble art; 'tis mean to rob a hen roost or a hen, but stealing thousands makes us gentlemen.*

On into M&S Gerry went with excitement and nerves colonising his insides in equal part. Two security guards — one tall, one short, both gormless — were standing just inside the door. Pay peanuts get monkeys is the thought that flashed through Gerry's mind as he passed them. Still, in this, game there was no room for complacency, especially not when the place concerned was covered by CCTV.

M&S on Princes Street wasn't as busy as you might expect on a weekday afternoon. However rather than out this down to the current state of the economy, Gerry put it down to the store's poor design and lay out. There just wasn't enough floor-space to fit comfortably the amount of stock that had been crammed in, and he hit the escalator on his way up to menswear on the third floor decidedly unimpressed.

Continuing on his way to menswear, Gerry thought about the irony of someone like him, paid handsomely to represent and defend shoplifters, going shoplifting himself. It brought a smile. Already enjoying the buzz of leading a double life, by the time he stepped off the escalator at menswear he was a man hopelessly addicted.

If the ground floor was crammed with stock, the third was positively jam-packed — rails of clothing standing almost back to back, interspersed with display cases and shelves of accessories. It was hardly a surprise when you considered that prior to the modernisation of this particular branch, there were two M&S stores in Princes Street, one selling women's clothes and accessories and this one devoted to menswear along with a furniture department and foodhall in the basement. The decision to close the women's store and cram both into one had obviously been taken to save money. But if in the process it meant that shopping here had been turned into an irritating experience, in the process alienating the customers, what was the point?

Gerry spent ten minutes or so floating around the place. He never bought menswear from here, but some of the accessories weren't bad and there were no alarms on many of the items. He knew this from a client he'd just represented.

Caught and convicted, the young man in question had a record for shoplifting that saw him sent down for six months last time. Not that it bothered him. On the contrary he'd boasted to Gerry about how much he made shoplifting, and from M&S in particular, telling Gerry he either sold the goods on for half price or else returned them and took the credit note, which could then be used as cash in any branch of M&S anywhere in the country.

Listening to him, it occurred to Gerry that if someone who dressed in a tracksuit and sported tattoos on his hands could make a living as a shoplifter, just imagine how successful someone like himself could be?

But, then, Gerry wasn't in it for the money, he was in it for the buzz.

When he came across the men's leather briefcases and holdalls against the wall in the far corner, he knew he'd found what he was looking for. A briefcase was the perfect item for what Gerry had in mind, as all you had to do was pick it up and walk out of the store with it in your hand while concealing the price tag in your grip.

But what about the briefcase he was already carrying? Wouldn't it look suspicious walking out the door with two on his person?

Not if he carried his own one over his shoulder it wouldn't, which is exactly what Gerry proceeded to do, deftly moving it from his hand to his right shoulder using the strap, after which, with his left hand, he lifted one of the brown leather briefcases off the peg on which they were hanging, first grabbing the price tag hanging from the handle by a piece of string and folding it in two inside his hand before placing said hand around the handle. It was now, without warning, that hesitation and doubt seeped into his thoughts.

When he'd walked out of John Lewis with the jump drive, he'd done so by mistake, distracted by the girl he was following at the time. But this time he was planning to walk out of M&S with a leather briefcase without paying for it on purpose, which only now did he realise was an entirely different proposition.

Standing there wrestling with his doubts and hesitation, he felt the first trickles of sweat running down his back underneath his white shirt. Shit, this is harder than I thought. How do they do it? How are they able to just pick things up and walk out with them as easily as they do?

'They' get caught, Gerry. 'They' have nothing to lose. 'You' do have something to lose. Think about your career, your reputation. Is it really worth risking both for a paltry £125 leather briefcase? Get a grip son. Get a…

"Hello sir, can I help you?"

Gerry turned to face the female sales assistant with a start. "Eh…no…I was just trying to make my mind up over which briefcase I prefer."

The lady looked at him, then at the briefcase in his hand. "Okay," she said after a pause, before turning and walking away again. As soon as she did Gerry replaced the briefcase on the peg and headed for the escalator. Halfway down it towards the second floor the two security guards he'd passed on his way in stepped on the up-escalator.

Shit!

As he approached them on his way down he looked straight ahead, determined not to look at them. But then it occurred to him that if he didn't make eye contact it might appear like he had something to hide. Christ, my head's bursting and here they come. Shit, they're staring at me. What should I do? What the fuck should I do?

Just as Gerry was about to pass the security guards on the other escalator a wave of calm washed over him and he looked straight at them, smiling like a man who had every reason to be confident about his place in the world.

The security guards looked at him impassively. Gerry knew instinctively that they were on their way up to the menswear department to watch him. The female sales assistant must have called them. She must have noticed me covering the price tag in my hand. That's what happens when you hesitate, he concluded. That's what happens.

Sure enough, when he stepped off the bottom of the escalator and took a quick look behind, the security guards were stepping on the escalator at the top to head back down again. Now Gerry knew for sure they were onto him and in response upped his pace as he stepped on the next escalator down to the first floor, followed by the last one down to the ground floor. He got off on the ground floor and, without looking back, walked smartly to the small set of steps leading up to the mezzanine level and then on along the passageway to the main exit and finally back out onto Princes Street.

Relief came on in waves as he started walking east, negotiating his way along the crowded pavement desperate to get off Princes Street and on to George Street, his natural habitat. By now the sweat was pouring out of him and he had to stop for a few seconds to wipe his forehead, which he did using his sixty-five quid Ferragamo tie. Having done so, on he went.

Upon reaching the sanctuary of George Steet, Gerry began to relax and his breathing began to return to normal. Continuing on his way, he was sure he'd lost his fucking marbles.

## 11
*Politics is war without bloodshed*

For Gareth Cairns the role of an MSP was becoming increasingly unbearable, not to mention untenable.

The ruling SMP executive's new spending proposals had just been released and the Scottish Labour Party leadership at Holyrood was now devoted to the task of picking them apart with the aim of ensuring as few as possible made it into legislation. To his consternation, the leadership had selected Gareth to sit on the ad hoc committee charged with the task of coming up with strong arguments against the Executive's proposed spending priorities over the coming year. This now meant him having to put in a full day's work — said work involving interminable meetings, reading through reams of documents, writing and submitting reports. Hitherto, Gareth had perfected the art of existing in the cracks, embracing the anonymity that comes with the relatively lowly status of a backbencher.

Up to now most of his colleagues had hardly had any contact with him apart from a perfunctory nod of the head whenever their paths crossed. Gareth's intention when becoming an MSP was to spend just one term in the role and use it as a launch pad to a far more lucrative career with one of the various companies and prominent businessmen he outdid himself in trying to help in some way or other; and always, it went without saying, for a modest commission.

Sadly for him, however, the way things were going with the recession, prospects for career advancement were looking increasingly bleak. Instead of attending a couple of lunches or dinners each week in the company of various individuals from the world of business and commerce, Gareth was lucky at this point if he attended one a month. It defied belief that things could be this bad, but bad they were and this to the point where if it didn't pick up soon he was looking at the very real possibility of having to consider putting himself up for re-election.

It is why he couldn't afford to take his new role less than seriously. With it, he'd stepped out of the shadows and was being watched and scrutinised by the party's hierarchy.

And right now there they were, arrayed around the table in Committee Room Number 10, the great and the good of the Scottish Labour Party, charged with upholding the great history and traditions of Labourism in Scotland. They were a sorry bunch of careerists, human evidence of how far the party had plummeted over the past decade or so.

The current leader of the Labour Party in Scotland, Iain Macleod, was such a nonentity it was rumoured his own mother had difficulty remembering his name. At this moment he was holding court, priming his fellow parliamentarians on the reason this new ad hoc committee had been set up and why it was deemed so important as part of Labour's fight back to power north of the border.

"So there you have it," Macleod addressed the meeting imperiously. "The task we have before us is absolutely fundamental to our prospects at the next election. We must begin to recover the ground we've lost over the past couple of years."

Macleod paused to take a sip of water, some of which escaped and dribbled down the front of his shirt.

"In our favour is an SNP Executive that grows evermore complacent, arrogant and out of touch. A cursory look at the spending proposals they've set out makes this clear. If you turn to page-54 and go the third paragraph," he continued, immediately triggering a flurry of activity as everyone picked up the document in front of them and turned to the relevant page, "you'll see there the proposal to change the name of the Scottish Executive to the Scottish Government."

Macleod placed his copy of the document back down on the table. "The cost of this alone — in terms of replacingexisting parliamentary and executive stationary and signage — is estimated, according to their own figures, to be forty-thousand pounds.

"But with this particular issue it's not so much the cost, it's the politics. For make no mistake, this is a clear attempt on the part of the SNP to divert attention away from the important work of the devolved Scottish Parliament onto the single issue of independence."

Gareth, listening, was fighting a losing battle to suppress a yawn. When it finally escaped, it drew the attention of the room, Macleod included, who proceeded to fix him with a cold stare. The resulting pause was pregnant with tension. Gareth now found himself being studied by ten of his fellow Labour MSPs, among them the six members of the shadow Scottish Executive.

"Mr Cairns, perhaps you would care to share your own analysis of this issue? You've obviously been paying close attention and have a clear grasp of the details."

The long comfortable sleep of anonymity was now not merely over where Gareth Cairns was concerned, it had morphed into him being thrown into the proverbial lion's den. The time had come for him to show some mettle or forever be considered dead wood; this was something he couldn't possibly afford to allow, lest he find himself unceremoniously deselected before the next election with no Plan B to fall back on.

Everything now was suddenly on the line — his ability to feed his growing credit card bills, his ability to shop and lunch at Harvey Nichols, his gym membership, nights out, his car: everything. In the time it took him to compute and process these these thoughts, Macleod concluded that he was a lost cause and returned his attention to the document, as did everyone else.

"In my opinion the entire strategy up to now has been misplaced," Gareth announced, the words leaving his mouth without having first been cleared by his brain. The meeting stopped and once again everybody's attention focused in on this hitherto anonymous backbencher.

"Really?" Macleod came back with a hint of sarcasm. "Perhaps you might care to elaborate."

"Okay, well, focusing on piddling issues such as the cost and political consequences of changing signs and stationary lacks ambition. If we expect the electorate to take us seriously as a putative ruling executive we first need to start taking ourselves seriously."

Macleod's face flushed red with anger at this remark, but Gareth was into it now and couldn't give a shit if Macleod's face turned bright green.

"The SNP has stolen our clothes," he continued, "and Alex Salmond, to give him his due, is a wily and experienced operator. He's continually wrong footed us on every major issue, to the point where we're now reduced to scouring everything they produce, every policy document, spending proposal and budget, looking for something, anything, to trip him up on.

"Being brutally honest, it's pathetic, and if we don't raise our game more than a few sitting in this room are looking at losing their seats come the next election."

People shifted uncomfortably in their seats. As for Iain Macleod, a lecture was the last thing he'd been expecting to spill from the mouth of a mere backbencher, someone who'd only been selected for this committee with the expectation that he'd keep his mouth shut and toe the line. Now here he was, this nobody, having the gall to upbraid the entire party and by implication its leader without fear or favour.

"I'm not sure I follow your argument," Macleod said. "And I'm not sure I like the hectoring tone in which you're making it either."

"That's because your chief concern is maintaining what little credibility you have left as leader," Gareth shot back, hitting him right between the eyes.

"I must say, this is completely out of order," Gillian Robertson, the party's deputy leader, opined.

Gareth shifted his gaze onto her. "All right," he said, "if you'd rather I remain silent, no problem, I'll be more than happy to oblige."

"No, wait," said Donald Anderson, another leading member of the shadow executive. "We shouldn't be afraid of criticism. I think we should allow him to continue and listen to what he has to say."

Nods of approval met this view, resulting in the anger on Iain Macleod's face giving way to foreboding. Sitting down, he filled his glass with more water from the jug in front of him and took a long drink.

"Okay," he said in a quiet voice, "if this is the consensus around the table then, please, go ahead."

Gareth took a sip of water from his own glass, straightened his tie and stood up. He took a few moments to comport himself — then he began.

What ensued was a forty minute speech in which Gareth Cairns laid out a vision for the party that would involve it charging the guns of the enemy armed with a new approach.

Gone would be the focus on minor issues. In its place would be a concerted attempt to inspire the country with an agenda for radical and progressive change, designed to kickstart the economy out of recession with a series of bold initiatives. Gareth urged his fellow Labour MSPs to start getting out into their constituencies with public meetings, appearances and meetings with people from all sectors of the community. It was time to put the Labour back into a Labour Party that in the eyes of its base had degenerated to the point where it was now more synonymous with spin and managerialism than passion and principle.

Where the words came from, Gareth Cairns would have been as hard placed as anyone to say. What passed between his lips was a stream of consciousness, with everyone present impressed by his eloquence and passion.

It would be remembered by every one of them for a long time to come, not least by Iain Macleod, who throughout sat in his chair shrinking with the horrible realisation that his leadership was inexorably headed for its end — unless, that is, he could bring this hitherto anonymous backbencher into the fold and win his support.

Yes, no doubt about it, for Gareth Cairns MSP the days of blissful anonymity were now well and truly over.

Mid-September announced its arrival with a demonstrable change in the temperature — all of a sudden cool where before it had been warm. That this change had taken people by surprise was evident in the persistence of many in continuing to dress in light summer clothing, as if putting up a last gasp resistance to the onset of autumn. At just before nine in the morning, midweek, George Street was alive with people heading to work in one of the myriad offices, banks, retail stores, hotels and cafes that ran its entire length.

Buses and cabs and private cars vied for space, with the usual morning congestion made exponentially worse by the hated tram works on Princes Street diverting even more traffic onto George Street. The result was it being far too crowded with traffic to make it the attractive destination for shopping, lunch, or coffee it was previously. Even the stentorian statues that punctuated the middle of the road at each junction all the way along George Street seemed to carry a more lugubrious aura than usual in response to the change in its fortunes.

At 9.30 am, the mayhem of the morning rush hour having eased off, Callum Wilson pulled up outside Browns bar and restaurant in George Street in a brand spanking new Mercedes four wheel drive. Black with tinted windows and black leather interior, the vehicle spoke of the luxury and quality with which Mercedes was inextricably linked.

Callum only picked up it from the dealership two days ago and a grin had hardly left his face since. He relished the looks of admiration and envy from other motorists when he pulled up alongside them at traffic lights, and the thought of the attention he was guaranteed to receive when he pulled up outside Tigerlily this coming Saturday night had him so excited it was near impossible to focus on anything else, including this morning's breakfast meeting with Simon his bank manager.

Before getting out of the car, he took a minute to check his teeth in the mirror. He'd just had them whitened but was unconvinced about the result as he studied them for the umpteenth time since. After a minute he pushed the sun visor back up, leaned across to the passenger side, popped open the glove and pulled out his blue disabled badge. With this he could park almost anywhere, including on yellow lines such as the one he was parked on now, without having to worry about landing a ticket from one of the army of parking attendants that swarmed the centre of Edinburgh on a daily basis.

That he did not qualify for a disabled badge was neither here nor there either. With Brian's connivance and credentials as a GP, he'd fabricated a chronic back condition in order to qualify. The fact he spent most days darting around the city checking up on tenants, viewing potential new property investments, and showing prospective buyers round properties he was selling, this was all the self-justification needed.

It wasn't something he fretted over to any great degree anyway, and with the nonchalance of a man for whom life couldn't be better, Callum Wilson stuck the badge on top of the dash, got out of the car and skipped across the pavement and on into Browns for breakfast with the one person in his life who mattered most.

"Hiya mate, sorry I'm a bit late," he announced upon arriving at the table and shaking Simon his bank manager's hand prior to sitting down across from him. "This bloody traffic's getting worse."

"Nice motor," his bank manager complimented him. "New?"

Callum nodding. "Yes, I just picked it up the other day."

"How's it drive?"

"Very well," Callum said, grinning. "Superb actually."

Simon Duncan was around the same age as Callum. He was married with five kids, which was reflected in his mode of dress and the paunch that sat over the waist of his trousers.

He and Callum enjoyed a tight relationship, up to the point where Simon had authorised the mortgage loans enabling Callum to expand to the point where he was about to invest in a new shopping centre development on the outskirts of the city. It promised to make him wealthy beyond anything he could ever have expected when he first started out fifteen years before with the purchase of a one-bedroom flat at the bottom of Leith Walk.

Quickly scanning his surroundings, taking in the chandeliers hanging from the ceiling, the well-considered layout and attractive combination of colours that had gone into the décor, it occurred to Callum that it might be an idea to stop off here on Saturday night for a cocktail before heading along the street to Tigerlily.

"So," Simon said, after the waiter tool their order, "how's things?""Things are good. Just put an offer in for that property out at Lasswade we discussed last week. I'm hoping to get it fifteen grand lower than the home report valuation."

Simon didn't say anything. Instead he looked down at the table with a circumspect look on his face.

"Is everything okay?" Callum inquired.

Simon looked. "I've got some bad news."

"What's that?"

"I've been made redundant."

The waiter arrived back at the table with their coffee, forcing Callum to wait before hearing the details, trying to get to grips in the few short moments that elapsed how Simon's fate might impact him.

"Fuck sake, why?"

"They carried out an audit when I was on holiday last month. I didn't know anything about it.

"They came across a few — shall we say irregularities — in relation to some of the mortgage loans authorised over the past year."

"You've made them a fortune. So what if you've cut a few corners here and there?"

"I wish it was as easy as that," he said. "It's not." "My overdraft facility?" Callum inquired, suddenly panicking. "It's still secure, yeah?" Simon looked at him, before lifting his cup and taking a sip of his coffee. "Isn't it?" Callum pressed.

"I'm not sure."

"What's that supposed to mean?"

"It means things have changed. We're in the midst of a recession. The banks are under pressure to account for every penny in and every penny out. Nobody can fart without the media getting to know about it in the current climate." He paused to sip his coffee. "It's bad."

Callum's heart sank further as this dire turn of events sunk into his brain.

"What about the shopping centre? Please tell me that the loan is still going ahead." Silence was his answer. "Bloody hell," Callum said, his appetite instantly gone. "Simon, mate, literally everything hinges on this. I've already shelled out 100 grand of my own money. If the bank pulls out now, I'll be fucked."

"All I can do is offer recommendations to whoever takes over."

"And who's that going to be?"

Callum took another sip of coffee, placed the cup back on the table, and shook his head. "Don't know yet."

Callum looked out of the window at his new car, then back to Simon.

"What about your dad?" Simon piped up. "Couldn't you approach him for a loan? If the worst comes to the worst, I mean."

"That's no longer an option."

"Why"

"It doesn't matter why," Callum repeated with anger creeping into his voice. Simon remained quiet, allowing Callum a few seconds to calm down. Having arrived for their breakfast meeting with his own problems at the forefront of his mind, he'd failed to fully appreciate the impact on Callum and others like him.

Yet faced with the onerous necessity of downsizing his entire existence in order to adapt to losing his job and the executive salary attached, who could blame him? If he failed to secure another role with a similar salary, his kids would have to be ripped out of their very expensive private education. He would also be forced to sell the large house in Morningside he'd only just moved into last year — and likely at a significant loss due to the impact of the recession on the property market. Last but certainly not least, he couldn't be sure if his marriage would survive.

"I'm sorry," Callum said, as if reading Simon's thoughts.

"You've got your own shit to deal with. It's just…fuck, what a fucking mess."

"Yes," Simon agreed in a hushed voice. "Everything has changed."

# 12

*Your children need your presence more than your presents*

The evening had been wonderful.

It began with a new adaptation of Shakespeare's Othello by the Royal Shakespeare Company at the Lyceum, then afterwards dinner and drinks at a new place on Queen Street.

By the time they left the restaurant they were tipsy and walked back to Brian's place arm in arm; Brian serenading her with a rendition of Rod Stewart's classic number, *Maggie May*, belting it out good style as they went; Tania laughing and telling him to shush and Brian in turn raising his voice and singing louder. Now they were in bed with Tania riding his cock as Brian rubbed cream on her tits.

They were interrupted by Brian's phone buzzing and flashing on the bedside table with an incoming call. At first Brian ignored it and continued with Tania grinding and riding him slow and deep. But no sooner did the phone stop buzzing than it started up again. It happened three times before it succeeded in breaking Brian's concentration and he stopped.

"Leave it," Tania said, breathless and desperate to carry on.

"I can't," Brian told her. "It might be work. Just gimme a sec."

Reluctantly, Tania got off him and Brian rolled over and picked up his phone. Trying to reach him was Gail. She'd left a voicemail. Brian quickly punched in his passcode to access the message. As soon as he heard it he scrambled out of the bed.

"I have to go," he announced, heading straight for the bathroom, where he flicked on the light and turned on the cold water tap. "Shit!" he repeated to himself. "Shit, shit, shit!."

"What's going on?" Tania said, sitting up. "What's wrong?"

Brian came to the door. "One of my kids has taken ill." He didn't wait for her reply and immediately retreated back into the bathroom to continue getting ready.

"Your kids?" Tania said. "I thought you didn't have any children?"

"You never asked," he called back, in-between splashing his face to sober himself up.

"Yes, I did."

Brian returned to the bedroom and began throwing on some clothes. "Did you?" he said while getting dressed in a rush. "Yes, you did. You were crying at the time."

Tania lay back down in the bed. "I don't believe this." Brian was putting his shoes on, sitting on the edge of the bed tying his laces. "Well," he said, "I'm afraid so." He got up from the bed and grabbed his jacket from the back of the door and threw it on. "And I'm sorry, but I really do have to go."

Five minutes later, driving as fast as was safe through pre-morning rush hour streets, Brian called Gail on his hands-free. "It's me. How is he? Any diagnosis?…No? Okay listen to me, calm down. It's going to be fine. I'll be there in fifteen….Yes, see you soon."

He ended the call and put his foot down. Guilt infused his entire being, guilt and self-recrimination, with everything banished from his mind apart from thoughts of his son, Harry. Brian Davison was at that moment a father and nothing else.

Exactly twelve minutes after ending the call with Gail, he was rushing along the corridor of the Sick Children's Hospital in Marchmont. At this hour it was near deserted and the echo of his feet striking the green marmoreal floor resounded like an ominous portent as he went. Even though himself a doctor and familiar with the protocol of never running in a hospital, he couldn't help himself and started running in the direction of the ward Gail informed him was where their son was being kept. Reaching the entrance to the ward, he almost ran into a nurse on her way out.

"Shit, I'm sorry," he blurted out. "I'm sorry."

"No running allowed," she admonished him.

"I'm here to see my son, Harry Davison. He was admitted earlier this evening."

The nurse, whose name was Cathy, had been in the profession for fifteen years experience and was thus well used to dealing with the kind of distress and anxiety she was dealing with now.

"Your son is in theatre," she said calmly. Quickly checking her watch, she continued, "He was taken down five minutes ago."

"Theatre? Christ, what…"

The nurse placed a reassuring hand on his arm. "It's only tonsillitis. It's okay."

"Oh thank God, I thought….Christ."

"He'll be kept in overnight for observation and probably be discharged tomorrow."

"Thanks," Brian said, calming down.

"You're the father?" the nurse went on.

Brian nodded. "Yes."

"His mother's already here."

"Where?"

"She's in the waiting room along the corridor. But…".

"But what?" Brian asked, stopping in his tracks after taking two steps in the direction the nurse had just pointed him in.

"Waiting room's just along the corridor to the right," Cath said, subtly shifting gear. "As soon as your son's out of theatre, we'll let you know."

The waiting room was brightly decorated in pastel colours. A liberal sprinkling of children's pictures and crayon sketches were hung up around the room, and in one corner a large box contained toys and games to keep any waiting children amused. In another corner a small kitchen area included a fridge, cupboards, a sink, cups and an electric kettle for making teas and coffees. Despite the attempt to create a relaxed and cosy atmosphere, the coruscating fluorescent lighting and hard plastic chairs belied it.

Sitting against the wall on the opposite side of the room from the door were Gail and Graham. Sitting on Graham's knee, snuggled up against him and sucking her thumb, was Brian's daughter Lucy. Brian stood by the door surveying the scene for a few seconds. Gail looked at him but didn't say anything, while Graham regarded him with his usual cold indifference.

"Hello" Brian said.

"Glad you could make it," Gail replied flatly. Awkwardly, Brian proceeded to take up position in a chair at the opposite side of the room. No sooner had he done so than Lucy got up off Graham's knee and ran over to him. Brian picked her up, placed her on his knee and hugged her tight.

A couple of hours later, driving home, Brian was mentally exhausted and emotionally drained. Harry's operation had gone without a hitch, yet even with the relief of knowing that his boy was okay, he was mentally shot. Perhaps it had been the atmosphere in the waiting room, the palpable tension that hung over the place as a result of the uneasy silence that had been like a brick wall lying between them. Brian had attempted to break the tension a couple of times, break the silence, but each attempt at civility had floundered on the rocks of Graham's hostility. What Gail sees in him, he thought, I don't know.

Deciding in the next breath that under the circumstances such trivialities were undeserving of his attention, he switched his thoughts to his kids. I need to spend more time with them.

I'll talk to Gail about having them over to stay with me more often. Taking them to school one day a week and having them on a Sunday afternoon is not enough. They need me in their lives more than that. No, that's not right, he thought again after a pause. It's not them who need me, I'm the one who needs them.

By the time he parked the car and entered his building on Abercromby Place, he was about done in. As he placed his key in his door, he hoped he wouldn't disturb Tania and that she was asleep. He wasn't in the mood to talk or try to explain. Not now; later maybe, but not now.

He went straight through to the bedroom. The bed was empty and made up. Lying on top of one of the pillows was a note. Brian walked over and picked it up.

> *I'm sorry honey, it was good while it lasted but I think it best if we both move on now. Take care, Tania xxx*

He read the note a couple of times then scrunched it up and chucked it in the small bin in the bathroom. He undressed, took a piss, washed his hands and brushed his teeth.

Climbing into bed the only thing on his mind were his kids. As long as they were all right nothing else mattered.

They'd arranged to meet at seven in the bar of the Scotsman Hotel on George IV Bridge. Gerry parked on Cockburn Street, running parallel behind George IV Bridge, and walked through the small shopping arcade connecting Cockburn Street to North Bridge and on down to the hotel on the left. He was on time and upon entering, scanned the bar to see if she was here yet. Good, he thought, noting that she hadn't yet arrived, I'll order a drink and grab a table before she gets here.

Her name was Shona and the only contact they'd had up to now was via three or four emails, followed by a couple of text messages when things progressed to the point where they'd exchanged numbers. Not once had they actually spoken over the phone. All Gerry knew was that she was blonde, slender and possessed a decent set of teeth. He also knew that she was Irish, as she'd put it on her profile, and also that she was 34 and worked as a legal assistant. Apart from that Gerry knew next to nothing about her. Nor she him, as it happened.

After weeks of trawling through profiles and sending winks and messages to countless women, Gerry had come round to the view that internet dating was a disappointment. He'd been on five dates and four of those he'd met hadn't looked as good in person as in their pictures. Only last week he met a 5'11" blonde fitness instructor from Livingston at a hotel in South Queensferry. She'd obviously put on considerable weight since the pictures she'd posted on her profile were taken. Rather than go through with it, Gerry tried to make a beeline for the door before she saw him. He was too late though; she spotted him and started heading over. Regardless, Gerry put his head down and kept going, sprinting for his car as soon as he got outside. He climbed in and wasted no time in putting the car into first and hitting the accelerator, keeping his head down as he sped past her at the hotel entrance out of the car park and away.

Back to tonight and just as he stepped up to the bar to order a drink, he happened to glance round at the door at the exact same moment his latest date walked in. Caught unawares, Gerry hesitated a second before stepping away from the bar to greet her. By the time he was halfway across the floor his stomach had already bounced off the floor in disappointment.

"Hi," he said in a contrived upbeat voice, offering his hand with a smile on his face, "how are you?"

"Pleased to meet you Gerry, I'm Shona," she said in a quiet voice while avoiding direct eye contact.

"Drink?" Gerry invited.

"Eh, yes…vodka and soda please."

They went up to the bar, Gerry inviting her to lead the way, and there he took over, stepping forward and ordering a vodka and soda for her and a small white wine for himself. The silence between them as the barman made up the drinks was painful. Conscious of her presence behind him, Gerry felt obliged to make conversation. It was just as he was about to, turning round to face her, that something snapped.

"Look," Gerry told her, "let's be honest, this isn't going to happen. I don't fancy you and I'm not prepared to waste my time pretending." Quickly turning back to the bar before she was able to respond, he addressed the barman. "Excuse me," he said, getting the guy's attention. "I'm sorry, but I'd like to cancel the order."

The barman had already made up the vodka and soda and was in the process of pouring the wine when Gerry made his request. He shot him a look of displeasure, but Gerry didn't notice, because by then he'd turned and taken his first steps in the direction of the door.

"You're very rude," Shona scolded him as he walked way, eyes registering that particular strain of anger born of humiliation.

"And you're very plain," Gerry came back, before continuing on his way out. Outside he took a breath and began striding down South Bridge in the direction of Princes Street. The strong breeze at his back propelled him forward; he felt confident and good about himself, and looking out over both sides of this long connecting bridge between Edinburgh's new and old towns, the spectacular and panoramic view fuelled his buoyant mood.

Confidence, he pondered, is what this shit called life is all about. Say what you mean and mean what you say.

In being honest back there Gerry Scott liberated himself from the agony of going through a date with someone he wasn't attracted to. From now on, he decided, I'm going to be assertive and direct when it comes to women. Enough of playing by the rules. Gerry Scott's the name and confidence is the game.

By the time he reached Princes Street his mind was made up on his next course of action. He was going to head straight along to M&S and prove to himself that he had the balls to pick up a leather briefcase and walk out the door without paying for it. He still had time — the store closed at eight on a Thursday evening — and thus there was nothing to deter him apart from fear.

Down with fear!

Princes Street was busy with late night shoppers, predominately of the low end variety it occurred to Gerry as he navigated his way along decidedly unimpressed. The Sale signs up in store windows were further evidence of the recession that had taken hold More than a few To-Let signs and billboards were also on display, confirming the ongoing degeneration of this once proud thoroughfare, which increasingly resembled a rundown high street.

Finally reaching M&S, Gerry strode in to the place absent of the hesitation or trepidation of his last visit. He knew exactly where he was going and confidently stepped onto the up-escalator, reaching mens on the third floor two minutes later, whereupon he sauntered over to the back wall, lifted a brown leather briefcase off the peg on which they were hanging, closed his hand around the price tag like last time, and turned and headed back over to the escalators.

Arriving back on the ground floor, he walked assertively along the main pathway to the exit doors and back out into Princes Street without so much as a glance back to check if he was being followed. On he went along the crowded pavement, experiencing a buzz such as he'd never experienced before.

## 13

*Push harder than yesterday if you want a different tomorrow*

Saturday morning and Gareth, Callum and Brian had converged on the gym at 11 sharp. They did four miles on the treadmill, then half an hour doing weight circuits, before finishing off with ten minutes doing core work before heading for the obligatory sauna, sunbed and shower. With his short and all-consuming relationship with

Tania now over, Brian was back to his old lifestyle and routine, which the inevitable jibes from Gareth and Callum notwithstanding was like putting on an old but very comfortable pair of trousers again. He was determined that where women were concerned never again would he allow himself to weaken and that going forward he would remain a committed player, concerned only with chasing pleasure and gratification.

As if to affirm the fact, when the three of them made their way over to Harvey Nichols for their regular stint of shopping and lunch after the gym, Brian treated himself to a two-button black Armani suit and a crisp white shirt by Paul Smith. Gareth picked up a couple of Fahri t-shirts, while Callum made do with a belt and matching cufflinks by Prada.

Shopping over, they headed for the elevators with their purchases and on up to the bar and restaurant on the top floor. After the usual banter with Pierre when they arrived, they settled down at their usual table by the window. Conspicuous by his absence was Gerry; it had been weeks since any of them last spoke to him and they were coming round to the possibility that he'd disappeared for good.

"Maybe he's met someone," Callum suggested as they worked their way through their regular salad variations.

"Na, not Gerry," Gareth said, taking a sip of mineral water. "Brian's the man for that malarkey."

"Oh yeah…I forgot," Callum said.

"Funny, very funny," Brian said.

Gareth said, "I just hope Gerry hasn't done anything mad such as…"

"Such as buy himself a decent suit?" Callum interjected.

"I'm serious," Gareth persisted. "Maybe we should call round the hospitals, just to be sure. He's gone off grid since that ugly incident at Lulu's."

"Calling round the hospitals might be an idea actually," Callum said. "Brian," he went on, "you haven't performed surgery on Gerry in the past couple of weeks and something's gone wrong, have you? Tell me, do they still cut people up and preserve them in jars for medical experiments?"

"Only your exes," Brian said.

Gareth's attention was suddenly drawn to the two girls who'd just sat down at the table on the other side of the bar. "Okay guys," he announced, "don't look now but we have ourselves a couple of hotties at three o'clock."

Brian and Callum looked over. "When I was at school," Gareth said, "three into two didn't go."

"Fear not my friend," Callum quipped, "even a blind chicken gets a piece of corn sometimes."

"You're talking to Gareth Cairns. If anybody's going to be left out of this equation, it'll be one of you two twits."

"Twits?" Callum said. "Did you just say twits?" Then, to Brian, "Did he just say twits?"

"Why Gareth, I'm shocked," Callum continued. "Such language. Whatever would your constituents say?"

"Constituents?" Brian said sarcastically. "What on earth are those?"

"That's a scurrilous accusation," Gareth said. "I'll have you know that I'm extremely conscientious when it comes to my duties as an MSP."

"Bullshit," Callum said.

"But nonetheless, spoken like a true politician," Brian quipped.

After a short pause, Callum decided to change the

subject. "So what about tonight then?" he asked. "How about Browns for dinner and then on to Tigerlily and the usual?"

"Sounds good to me," Gareth agreed.

"Brian?" Callum said. "That sound all right to you?"

"If I'm honest, I think it's about time we tried somewhere different?"

"Such as?"

"I don't know," Brian shrugged. "Glasgow?"

"Glasgow?" Gareth said in a tone of unalloyed distaste.

"Why would anyone ever want to go to Glasgow?" Callum said.

"What's wrong with Glasgow?" Brian said. "The nightlife's meant to be good."

"Are you out of your mind?" Callum asked him.

"No, I'm not. I'm just suggesting we try something different."

"Brian,' Gareth said, "Glasgow's full of Glaswegians. They're not like us."

"All right, maybe Glasgow isn't the answer," Brian said, accepting defeat. "I still think we need to try somewhere different though. This shit is getting old."

Callum glanced over at Gareth then back to Brian and said, "You're depressed. Your heart's been broken. We understand. We feel your pain."

"And you're looking for something, anything, to distract you from that pain," Gareth followed up.

"Ever thought about counselling?" Callum said next, determined to keep it going.

Brian looked at the two of them smiling back at him. "All right, you asked for it, he confidently announced. "A twenty says I pull first tonight."

"Make it fifty and you've got a bet."

Some six hours later they were in their usual spot in the back corner of Tigerlily by the main bar. From here they were able to take in the entire seating area, along with much of surrounding standing room before and beyond.

Brian, determined to make good on the bet they'd made earlier, had reason to feel confident —dressed to the nines as he was in his new Armani suit and Paul Smith shirt. Callum and Gareth had both opted for a casual look: Callum in an off-brown T-shirt by Issay Miyake, brown Hackett sports jacket, and dark denim jeans by 7 For All Mankind: Gareth in a pair of Donna Karan grey canvas trousers, light blue sweater by John Smedley, a thin navy three quarter length coat by Versace, and Diesel trainers.

After they'd got their drinks, spent a few minutes engaging in some light hearted banter, it was time to look around the place and see what and who was cooking.

"You ready with that fifty?" Callum said as he zeroed on a couple of girls standing by one of the pillars on the other side of the bar.

"I'm ready to receive one," Brian replied, his attention on the Asian girl seated in a group eating dinner in one of the booths, hoping she would notice him and reciprocate.

"You guys obviously like to throw your money away," Gareth said. "You taken a gander at me lately? I'm the man who put the bubble in the bubblebath."

Callum spotted a group of girls making their way to the bar. The taller one immediately registered on his radar and he decided to move in. "Anybody got a spare blue one? I forgot to bring one tonight."

Gerry went into his pocked, fished out his wallet, brought out a blue kamagra tablet and handed it over.

"All right gentlemen," Callum announced. "Let battle commence."

Gareth shook his head in a gesture of disdain, watching him go. "He's making mistake. You should never commit your forces into battle too soon. I read that in Sun Tzu's classic work, *The Art of War*."

Brian, like Gareth, had his focus on Callum just as he arrived in front of the girl. "Here we go and…boom! Crash and burn," he declared in response to the sight of him being unceremoniously rejected with an imperious wave of the hand.

"Hard lines, Callum," Gareth said when he returned, suitably chastened. "Don't worry son, the night's still young."

"Yep," Brian chimed in, "plenty of time to wrack up more knock-backs."

It was now that the guys noticed Gerry making his way towards them through the bar.

"Just when we were starting to think you were dead," Gareth said, shaking his hand when arrived in their company.

"About time too," Callum said, shaking his hand next.

"What are you drinking, Gerry?" Brian asked him. "Champagne?"

Gerry nodded his assent and Brian went to the bar to fetch another glass. While he was away, the others noticed that Gerry's attention was elsewhere.

"What's the matter?" Callum asked. "Bored with us already?"

"I'm meeting someone here tonight," Gerry said.

"Meeting someone?" Gareth replied. "Who? Not James Traynor, I hope?"

"For your information, I have a date."

"Now this I have to see," Callum quipped.

"Me too," Gareth agreed enthusiastically.

Brian had returned from the bar with the glass and was pouring Gerry some champagne. "Don't listen to them," he said. "They're just jealous." He handed Gerry his drink. "Where did you meet her, anyway?"

Gerry took a sip of champagne. "Online."

Gareth had just taken a sip of his own drink and immediately spat it out laughing. Callum burst out laughing at the exact same moment, while Brian only just managed to hold it together.

"Online?" Brian asked, seeking confirmation.

"What's wrong with that? It's the done thing nowadays."

Gareth and Callum were still tickled by it.

"What time are you supposed to be meeting her then?" Brian asked Gerry next, amused at the sight of him searching the bar, looking for her while checking and re-checking his watch.

"Round about now," Gerry told him.

"Is this a first date?"

"Third."

Callum, pulling himself together, said: "What's she like?"

"Wait and see."

"Wait and see?" Gareth said. "I've got work on Monday morning."

Suddenly, Gerry's face lit up. "There she is now," he announced, waving to a girl he'd just spotted in the crowd.

The girl in question was five-ten, slim, with pale skin and long straight red hair. As she made her way through the bar every man in the place, and quite a few of the ladies, stopped to take a look.

She was stunning and Gareth and Callum were no longer laughing.

Reaching Gerry, she gave him an enthusiastic kiss and Gerry responded by putting a confident arm round her waist.

"Guys, this is Heather," he proudly announced.

"Hello, it's nice to meet you," Heather addressed them with a smile, before giving each of them a polite handshake. After doing so, she turned her attention back to Gerry, nibbling his neck with her hair falling over her face in the process.

The others were speechless. In fact more than speechless, they were agog.

"Right," Gerry said, "we have a table booked at Browns, so I guess I'll speak to you guys later." And with that he began leading his date away by the hand.

"Bye," Heather said with a little wave as they left.

"Enjoy your evening," Brian told her.

As soon as they were gone, Brian turned to Callum and Gareth, both of whom were still struggling to wrap their heads around what just took place.

"The tables have been well and truly turned.

Gareth said, "I'm signing up to this internet dating malarkey first thing in the morning."

"Absofuckinglutely," Callum remarked. "If he can do it so can we."

"Now-now gentlemen, credit where credit's due," Brian said. "The man has turned things around and I say good on him.

"Anyway," he continued, "what say you we depart this place and take our custom elsewhere?"

## 14

*It hurts to breathe because every breath I take proves I can't live without you*

The guys left Tigerlily and started heading east along George Street, having decided to have a drink in the Living Room before heading back to Lulus. It was a cool night, too cool to be out without a jacket, yet many out walking and cavorting along George Street at this time on a Saturday night were exactly that while too inebriated to care. As the guys moseyed along the street, Brian was trying but failing to keep thoughts of Tania at bay. Despite trying to banish her from his mind since receiving her note telling him it was over, it was futile. Reverting back to the life of the single man about town he'd led prior to meeting this woman had only succeeded in emphasising the extent to which he missed her.

Back engaging in the usual banter and antics with the guys, trawling the same bars and clubs frequented by the same faces, had produced a clawing sense of despair and futility. Is this it, was the question colonising his mind as he walked along a busy George Street with Callum and Gareth? Is this really all there is?

The latter were blissfully unaware of the inner turmoil Brian was experiencing. They were just delighted to be out on the town on another Saturday night and, try as he might, Brian couldn't help but take a dim view.

They'd been friends now almost three years; Brian meeting them after he split from Gail and began becoming a regular face in and around Edinburgh's nightlife. Back then he would venture out by himself. And even though in the beginning it wasn't very comfortable — trying to fit in and appear at ease but feeling self-conscious — like anything in life he got used to it. Anyway, what was the alternative? He was single, living by himself, and given that all his friends back then were in couples, his only other option was staying in and spending his weekends feeling sorry for himself.

What started as a casual acknowledgement of Gareth and Callum whenever they crossed paths while out and about progressed to a bit of banter and a few words of small talk. It wasn't too long before they exchanged numbers and Brian began hooking up with them — initially for nights out, then also for lunch and the gym. When Gerry stepped into the picture not long after, the group was complete.

But now three years down the line (Christ, three years, where had the time gone?), Brian was questioning everything. His time with Tania had provided him with a glimpse of another life, one that consisted of more than punishing himself in the gym in the quest for a perfect body, skin treatments and regular sunbeds; more too than shopping for designer clothes and spending weekends on the hunt for female attention and false intimacy of casual sex. Increasingly, despite trying to pretend otherwise, he wanted more, much more, with Tania responsible for catalysing feelings that wouldn't go away.

Later, standing in Lulus watching the drunken antics of everyone around him — Gareth and Callum off chatting to women in different parts of the club — Brian was no longer able to keep up the masquerade and he put down his drink and left.

He did so quietly, without bothering to let Gareth or Callum know. The way he was feeling he didn't want to speak to anyone, imbued as he was with an overwhelming urge to get back to his flat and shut everything and everybody out.

As he walked along George Street, this grand thoroughfare built during the heady days of the Scottish Enlightenment in the mid to late eighteenth-century and now reduced to a dystopia where every weekend the drunken antics of men and women unfolded — people on whom the neoclassical architecture, monuments and statues were completely lost — revulsion filled his being. His eyes fell upon the young guy sitting on the ground with his back to the wall of the bank adjacent to a cash machine.

As with the majority of people walking past, along with most of those in the queue waiting to take money from the machine, Brian rarely paid notice to the rising number of homeless people punctuating Scotland's capital. They were to all intents invisible, a status only raised to that of minor irritant whenever they had the temerity to call attention to their existence with a request for spare change.

Tonight, heeding this call for the first time in years, Brian reached into his pocket, fished out his wallet and handed the man a crisp twenty pound note. He walked on with a hearty "God bless you" ringing in his ears while questioning a society that allowed so much suffering and despair to exist alongside so much opulence and ostentation and have the arrogance to believe that this was the best of all possible worlds.

By the time he reached Abercrombie Place and home he felt sufficiently drained by the night's events to undress and go straight to bed. Lying there in the dark, thoughts of Tania vied for supremacy in his consciousness with thoughts of the young homeless guy he encountered earlier on George Street. The search for meaning in love and in suffering was, he was starting to realise, the search for the answer to a simple question.

Why?

Friday morning and in her room at The Balmoral,

Tania was packing the last of her things with the porter standing just inside the door, waiting patiently to take her bags as son as she was finished.

"Okay," Tania told him, "that's it."

The porter stepped forward with a dutiful smile, took the bag and placed it on the trolley with the rest of her luggage, then began pushing it in the direction of the elevators at the end of the corridor. Tania put on her coat and picked up her bag. Before leaving, she took a moment to look around the room, reflecting on what was and what might have been.

Five minutes later, the elevator arrived on the ground floor with its usual ping and Tania emerged with the porter and her luggage. While he headed for the exit and the cab waiting outside with her luggage, Tania made her way over to reception to check out with Michael, wearing a smile on his face as she approached.

"Okay honey," she addressed him warmly. "That's me, checking out."

"Certainly," Michael said while on his computer typing . "I'll print out your invoice."

Michael finished typing and disappeared into the back office to fetch the invoice from the printer. Moments later he returned and placed the invoice on top of the desk. "A copy will also be emailed to you," he informed her.

"You're so efficient," Tania told him as she removed a credit card from her purse and handed it over.

Michael produced the machine, slid the card in the slot, typed in the amount, then spun the machine round for Tania to punch in her pin. This she did and moments later the payment went through and out popped a receipt. Michael removed it, clipped it to the top of the invoice and handed it back to her along with her card.

"Great," Tania said, taking the credit card back from him and putting it back in her purse. She then proceeded to remove some cash.

"Thanks, but that's not necessary."

"No-no, please…take it."

Michael relented, took the money and placed it in his pocket. "Thank you, you're very kind."

"You know something," Tania told him, "I'm gonna miss Edinburgh."

"And Edinburgh's going to miss you."

Tania laughed. "You're so sweet."

"Give my regards to New York."

"You should visit sometime."

"If I do I might not come back."

Unfolding outside was the usual scene of heavy traffic and bustling pavements either side of Princes Street. Tania didn't tarry and descended the stone steps to the street and straight over to her cab; the porter having already placed her luggage in the boot with the driver helping him and Fred the hotel's faithful doorman standing with the rear door open. Just before getting in she handed the porter and Fred the requisite tip; Fred hitting her with a friendly salute in response as she climbed in. He closed the door then signalled to the driver, who responded by indicating right, pulling out and driving off as soon as the traffic allowed.

Exactly thirty-seconds later the place outside the hotel just vacated by Tania's cab was taken by another cab pulling up into it. Out of the back jumped Brian, his face a study in determination as he proceeded to bound up the steps two at a time, past Fred at the entrance, on inside and straight over to reception.

"Okay Michael where is she? And this time I'm not taking no for an answer."

"Oh, you again."

"Yes, me again. You can call security, you can even call ghostbusters — I'm not leaving until I see her."

"That's very interesting," Michael said. "However, as much as I'd love to put you to the test, she just left."

"What?"

"I believe she's booked on a 10am flight to JFK."

"God sake, why didn't you tell me?"

"I just did."

Brian spun round and sprinted straight for the door. Watching him, Michael could only smile and shake his head.

The cab carrying Tania was wending its way through the centre of Edinburgh. As it did she looked out the window at people going about their lives, struck by the difference in intensity between New York and Edinburgh, by how the lack of history over there sat in contrast with the sheer weight of it here.

Then she thought about Brian and their month together — of how she'd allowed herself to believe that in this

Scottish guy had lain the happiness that was missing in her life. How silly of her? How silly and how irresponsible? Never again, she determined. Never again would she let her guard down where men were concerned. No, it was time to wise up, get back to New York and refocus on her career.

But then?

Stop it, she berated herself. Stop this nonsense. He was a distraction, is all. Nothing more than a distraction.

Now it's over.

In the back of his own cab — the one he'd jumped straight into outside the Balmoral — Brian couldn't sit still. Through the heavy traffic heading west in the direction of the airport, he willed it forward, cursing every traffic light, roundabout and junction impeding its progress.

Edinburgh Airport was the usual carnival of commuters and business people rushing to catch flights to cities throughout the British Isles, Europe and beyond, forming a fungible sea of dark suits. Tania entered the departures terminal and made her way to check in. The time was approaching nine and she hurried to join the queue before it grew any longer.

Standing there — and despite herself — she experienced a surge of regret at the thought of what might have been. How long had it been since her marriage ended? Three years. Three years had elapsed and it frightened her to think how much she'd grown used to being on her own.

The handful of dates she'd been on had been disappointing, involving insecure men carrying more baggage than your average transatlantic flight. But then again perhaps, just perhaps, the problem lay with her and not the men she was meeting.

Maybe she was just too fussy and fastidious. Maybe it was time she just accepted that the kind of men she'd been meeting and rejecting up to now were the only kind out there.

She checked in and made her way to the departure gate on the first floor. Clutching her carry-on bag she stepped on the up-escalator, attracting more than a few second looks from male admirers as she went. Even in a conservative navy blue trouser suit she stood out, though at that precise moment her sombre mood left her decidedly underwhelmed by any attention she was receiving.

Just as she reached the first floor, Brian entered the terminal through the large sliding doors, eyes roving left and right over the sea of people. To his right was the escalator leading up to the departure gates. He scoured the ground floor one more time before stepping on the escalator and walking up it two steps at a time to the consternation of those he passed. Reaching the top he turned and surveyed the entire length of the concourse to the security gate leading to Departures. Three quarters of the way along, Tania was walking steadily in that direction.

"Tania!"

Brian's voice filled the concourse and instantly drew the bewildered attention of everyone within earshot. Oblivious to everything except Tania in the distance, Brian started running.

"Tania! Wait!"

Having reached the security gate, Tania was just about to pass through when she heard her name being called. She turned to see Brian running towards her waving like a madman, dodging in and out of people barring his path and and being met with shaking heads and furrowed brows. Upon reaching her he had to take a few seconds to catch his breathe; Tania struggling to get to grips with the situation as he did.

"Listen to me," he began between breaths, "don't go. We can fix this. We can sort it out. I love you. I need you." Tania was still trying to get over the shock of his arrival never mind digest his words. It seemed a long time elapsed, though in truth it was only a few moments, before she told him, "You lied to me."

"No…I mean, yes," Brian said. "Yes, I did lie to you. But only because I didn't want to hurt you. I saw how the mention of children affected you. I…"

"Don't take me for a fool," Tania interrupted him in a voice shaking with emotion.

Brian took a deep breath as the magnitude of the exchange, the realisation of what was at stake, sunk in.

"Look, Tania," he said, "whatever the problem is we can fix it. I love you. I'm serious. I've never felt like this about anyone.

"And yes," he went on, drawing closer, "I do have children. I have two and love them dearly. But that doesn't mean I can't have more." Listening to this, Tania filled up. "We could have our own family," he continued, spurred on by ever-increasing waves of hope. "We could be happy together."

Having just committed everything he had, every scintilla of sincerity and meaning he possessed, Brian waited for her response. Only a few feet separated Tania from the security gate and the end of something, and she stood there fighting to control emotions now swirling around inside, purposely averting her eyes down to the floor lest she lost it and broke down.

Managing to collect herself, she looked up at him again. "You don't get it, do you?"

Brian grabbed her hand in his. "Then tell me. All I want is to make you happy."

She removed her hand and said, "I don't even know if I can have children anymore. The doctors told me…my baby died. Now I…" She took a couple of seconds before continuing: "My husband left me. He told me he would love me no matter what and…and he lied." She sobbed. "He lied to me too."

In the pregant pause that ensued, Tania shook her head in pain, then turned and walked on through the security gate.

It was a broken and miserable man that emerged from the main departures terminal at Edinburgh Airport.

After Tania left him at the security gate, Brian hung around hoping she would have a change of heart and return. But as seconds turned to minutes the realisation she was gone and wasn't coming back sunk in. Arriving with this realisation came a dark wall of misery in his heart that made every breath painful. Accepting defeat, he began a long mournful walk back along the concourse to the escalators.

On his way down to the exit everything was reduced to a blur. Stunned, traumatised, mesmerised, Brian right then was all of those things, and stepping outside the sudden change in temperature along with the awning of black cloud that had formed in the sky above went completely unnoticed. The noise and mayhem of the traffic, of buses and cabs pulling in and out, of people being dropped off or picked up, couples parting and reuniting, none of it registered as he trudged lugubriously in the general direction of home. An hour later he was still walking, rejecting the option of taking a cab or even a bus. Despite the rain, which had started falling heavily, he kept going, placing one foot in front of the other as in a funeral march.

The vibration of his phone with an incoming text sparked a sudden surge of hope that it might be Tania texting to ask him to come back to the airport where she was waiting for him. He stopped walking, reached into his pocket, fished out the phone and read the message.

It was from Gail.

> *Just reminding you to pick up the kids from school today. Remember, it's their half day.. Oh the joys. x'*

Brian placed the phone back into his pocket and resumed walking. By now he was soaked through.

It took him another hour and a half to reach the school gates, having finally opted to take a bus back into Edinburgh after walking for an hour in the rain. He took up position beside other waiting parents. All of them were carrying umbrellas and cast sideways looks in his direction at the state of him standing there drenched with no protection from the rain. He didn't care, in fact didn't even notice, and instead just stood waiting patiently for the children to emerge.

Just before noon the bell sounded and seconds later a tidal wave of excited, noisy kids exploded from the building and swarmed in the direction of the gates. Among them were Lucy and Harry, running down the path waving at their dad as they came. When they got close, they both recoiled at the sight of him.

"Daddy!" Lucy told him off. "You're all wet!"

"I know sweetheart."

Lucy handed him the pink umbrella her mother had packed her off to school with earlier that morning. Brian took it, put it up and held it over his head. "Come on guys," he said. "Let's go and grab some lunch."

"Can I have chips?" Harry asked as they set off down the street.

"You can have whatever you want, pal."

"Daddy, can I have ice cream?" Lucy said, grabbing his free hand.

"Of course you can. What flavour?"

"Strawberry," she announced emphatically.

"Chips and strawberry ice cream it is then," Brian said. And on they went along the street, Brian carrying Lucy's pink, plastic umbrella over his head completely unconcerned as to how he looked.

They decamped to a small café in Stockbridge and sat down at a table in the corner. Brian sipped a skinny latte and watched the kids tuck into their food. His mind was elsewhere, trying manfully but failing to come to terms with the shock of losing Tania. The place was busy with the usual lunchtime trade, yet he felt as though he was sitting in a dark tunnel, isolated and alone. The knowledge that he was feeling like this in the company of the kids piled a layer of guilt on top of the despair he was already struggling to cope with.

When the cab pulled up outside the house a couple of hours later the kids were glad to be home and out of the rain. Gail opened the front door just as they came running up the path, Brian following in their wake with the rain still battering down. "Hey, you're all wet," Gail said as they came running into the house.

Brian trudged in last, wiping his feet on the mat.

"My God," Gail said in response to the sight of him.

He looked at her with a blank resigned look on his face. Moments later, Graham emerged from the living room.

"Okay, look, I best be off," Brian stammered uncomfortably.

"No daddy, stay," said Lucy, grabbing his hand on the back of a sudden wave of sympathy. Brian looked at Gail in response, shifting his weight awkwardly.

"Daddy can't stay, darling," Gail said, stroking Lucy's head. "Maybe next time."

"Right kids, come on then, "Graham said. "Let's get you upstairs and dried off.

The children failed to respond to Graham's command and Gail stepped in, her voice impatient. "Go on," she said. "Do as you're told." Instead, the kids moved closer to Brian, grabbing on to him with a sad but determined look on their faces. Graham glared at Gail and disappeared back into the living room.

"I better go," Brian said, feeling responsible for the awkwardness of the situation. "Bye guys," he said to the kids. "Be good and I'll see you next week."

"No," Harry said, his mouth curling up as he got ready to start crying. "I want you to stay."

Brian bent down to talk to them both. "Look, I can't today because I have to go to work. Maybe next time, all right?"

"Promise?" Lucy said.

Brian shot a look up at Gail, before turning back to Lucy.

"I said maybe. Now be a good girl and do as mummy says."

Lucy and Harry turned and headed up the stairs. Meanwhile, Gail's face and body language betrayed the fact there was something bothering her.

"You okay?" Brian inquired. "What's wrong?"

Gail took a deep breath. "Look, this isn't easy but…"

"But what?" Brian said after a short pause. "What is it?"

"I was going to ask if you'd mind giving me back the house key."

Brian took a moment. "The key?"

"It's…well, things are difficult. You know, with…" Gail said this while moving her head and her eyes in the direction of the living room.

Brian went into his pocket and pulled out his keys. After locating the one in question, he removed it from his keyring and handed it over.

"I'm really sorry," Gail said, looking at him standing there soaked to the skin.

Brian nodded and was about to turn to head back out the door when she stepped forward and gave him a hug. He was able to force a smile in response. Now it was Gail's turn to be concerned.

"Are you all right?" she said.

"I'm fine," he said, nodding his head. "I'll speak to you soon."

He opened the front door, stepped out and walked up the path, through the gate and off along the street.

It was still raining.

Not only outside but also inside.

Brian Davison, at that moment, was a desolate and devastated man.

## 15

*The process by which banks create money is so simple that the mind is repelled*

It was a cold but clear day and keen to make a good impression with his new bank manager, Callum opted to wear his dark grey suit by Kenzo along with a crisp white Prada shirt and navy Burberry raincoat.

The meeting was being held in the manager's office at the bank's headquarters on St Andrew Square, just up the street from Harvey Nichols, where he'd arranged to meet one of his ex's for lunch afterwards. Deciding to dispense with the car, he called a cab. It got him there in fifteen minutes from his luxury flat in Murrayburn and he walked into the grand Georgian building trying to convince himself that everything was going to be okay.

And why wouldn't it be? Over the past few years his business had generated a lot of money for the bank and it seemed only right that during these uncertain times the bank should stand by him until the economy picked up and everything returned to normal.

But then what about the exchange he had with Simon at Browns a few weeks back? Hadn't he informed him that everything had changed, that Callum could no longer count on the bank's support and the generous lending arrangements he'd enjoyed hitherto? Hadn't he told him that every business and personal overdraft was now under review, that the bank was looking to reduce its overdraft commitments substantially over the next six months or so? Hadn't he told him all that? Yes, he had, which is why as he approached the reception desk just inside the door, Callum felt his surroundings close in on him like a giant man-trap.

Cameron Ogilvy, the bank's new manager, arrived to collect him from the waiting room ten minutes later. Callum's initial impression was that here was a man who lived solely for his career.

He appeared a good few years older than Simon, and judging by his slightly rotund figure and a very sober and very plain looking suit, Callum quickly deduced that the two of them didn't share much in common, something that in his experience acted as a barrier when it came to forging a business relationship.

As a result, following him up the grand marble staircase to his office, the walls covered in austere paintings and portraits of the bank's previous incumbents, a strong sense of foreboding dominated his being. This bastard is about to cut my balls off, he thought ruefully as he climbed the stairs behind him. I just know he is. I feel it.

How things had changed. The last time Callum was here, he and Simon had shared a bottle of Moet Chandon and a gram of charlie in his office prior to heading out on the town. That was just at the start of the year, just after Callum sold his last property for a healthy profit. Who could have predicted the extent to which things would change in just the few short months since then?

Ogilvy showed Callum into his office and the leather chair on the other side of his desk. The desk, Callum noted, was the epitome of tidiness.

"Can I get you something to drink — tea, coffee, fruit juice perhaps?"

Callum asked for a glass of water, which Ogilvy fetched from a jug on the wall unit behind the desk. He gave Callum the water then sat down and opened the file that was lying on top of the desk.

"So," Ogilvy began after a few seconds, "I've had a look at your various accounts."

Exactly one and a half hours later Callum emerged from the bank like a man who'd been hauled before a firing squad and granted a reprieve a moment before the order to fire is given. His business overdraft was being frozen, pending a review, but the more important and salient point was that his personal overdraft of fifteen grand a month would remain as is for now. This meant that his lifestyle could continue in the same vein to thus spare him the ignominious fate of having to cut back. It also meant he could leave the money he had stashed away in a Jersey bank account, which the tax man didn't know about, untouched.

Walking out the gate, turning right and heading down the street in the direction of Harvey Nichols, he was filled with gladness, imbued with that most addictive of narcotics known as relief. Arriving at the bank his steps had been heavy. Now, emerging, he wasn't so much walking as gliding across the pavement, moving in and out of the other pedestrians with the nimble footwork of a young Cassius Clay in his pomp.

He'd arranged to meet Daphne for lunch and was half an hour early, thus leaving him time to browse menswear and perhaps pick up a new shirt to celebrate his good fortune.

With this in mind, he breezed in through the main entrance with a cheery greeting to Alan, the doorman, and on through cosmetics to the up-escalator. On nodding terms with a few of the girls working in cosmetics, he revelled in the attention his presence was attracting from them. On the escalator, he took the opportunity to look at himself on the mirror, oblivious to the fact he was being watched by someone five steps behind. Callum's browse began in the Nicole Fahri section. There was nothing here that he hadn't seen already, but that didn't matter; he still enjoyed the act of looking at the items laid out on the tables and hung up on the rails, displayed to make them appear as attractive and desirable as possible.

Losing himself in this bubble of luxury was an escape from the monotony of making money, of buying and selling properties, a process that left him cold and decidedly unfulfilled. He enjoyed spending money not making it, and Harvey Nichols is where he and the rest of the guys preferred to spend theirs.

After five minutes in the Fahri section he meandered over to Prada, passing through lesser labels such as Diesel and Hugo Boss to get there. Callum wasn't a big Prada fan, unlike Brian who swore by it, but he was content to take a look anyway.

What put him off Prada was the cut of the suits and coats — a little on the feminine side for his taste. Plus its distinctive red stripe had, just like Burberry check, come to be increasingly associated with ned culture. Burberry had even abandoned its check a few years back in an attempt to end this unfortunate association. Prada, it occurred to Callum, might have to do the same with regard to its iconic red stripe if they too wanted to maintain brand status.

By now there was fifteen minutes left before his lunch date. He hadn't seen Daphne in months and was looking forward to finding out if there might be an opportunity to get her into bed this afternoon. The last time they slept together was at the Orocco Pier Hotel in South Queensferry.

Callum remembered it well. Her husband was away at the time and Callum took the opportunity to book a room with a view out to the River Forth and the bridge in the near distance. They had drinks and dinner and then repaired to the room upstairs for a night of sex. They'd kept in touch since then via the odd text. Daphne had been the one to suggest they meet for lunch, which to Callum could only mean her husband was leaving town for a few days and that another rendezvous was on the cards.

Luckily, he knew exactly what he was after today — a Paul Smith white shirt — and picking one in his size from the table he marched over to the cash desk and handed it over to Oliver, one of the sales staff, who rung him up, bagged it and handed it back along with the receipt. Callum received his goods with a smile, bid Oliver a hearty farewell, then headed for the elevators on his way to the fifth floor for his lunch date.

Arriving there a minute later, he was quickly and efficiently seated at the regular table by the window he usually shared with the guys. It was Pierre's day off today, but that didn't matter because Callum was known by the staff and treated accordingly.

In no time he had a glass of ice cold mineral water in front of him, which he sipped as he moved his eyes between the menu and the elevators in anticipation of Daphne's arrival. The man walking through the restaurant in his direction Callum failed to notice until he was at his table, sitting down in the seat opposite.

"Eh…I'm sorry, that's seat's taken."

"Aye, I know," the man said. "I know it's fucking taken."

Callum's eyes moved beyond the man in a frantic search for a member of staff, anybody to come to his rescue. The intensity emanating from the eyes of this interloper, the feral energy he emitted, left Callum in no doubt that his was a hostile presence. "I'm sorry," Callum said, clearing his throat. "Do we know each other?"

"We do now," the man said, leaning forward. He then picked up the knife at his place and held it up to Callum's cheek. "You ever make a move on my wife again, cunt, and I'll cut ye wide open." He paused to let the message sink in. "Understand?"

Eyes wide with terror, Callum's throat suddenly felt as dry as the sun. "Y-your wife?"

"Daphne. You'd arranged to meet her for lunch here today, didn't ye?"

"Well, I eh…."

"Don't you fucking dare deny it."

"Excuse me, is everything all right?"

David, the duty manager, was standing by the table, his attention like that of everyone else in the place drawn by the commotion.

Without taking his eyes off of Callum, Daphne's husband said, "Aye, everything's fine pal. I was just leaving."

And with that the guy stood up, turned and walked off in the direction of the elevators. "What was that all about?" David asked Callum, whose normally tanned features were chalk white.

"That? Oh, just some guy who thought he recognised me." He looked up at David and forced a smile. "Anyway, you know what, I think I'll give lunch a miss today. I, eh… I completely forgot I've got an appointment at two." Callum got up. "Sorry."

And with that Callum too headed off, walking through the restaurant accompanied by the eyes of everyone in the place.

Deciding to take the stairs instead of the lift in order to place more time between himself and his assailant, he did so sick with fright and humiliation. Nothing like this had ever happened to him before and he was rattled.

Rather than head straight out of the place, he walked back into the menswear department just in case Daphne's husband was waiting outside. This time he only pretended to browse; his interest in the clothes zero as he struggled to maintain a calm front.

As he wandered across to where the Armani suits were displayed, he received a text. At first he was reluctant to look at it (it might be him), but curiosity won out and he opened it.

*lol, behind you.*

Callum turned with his heart palpitating to be met by the sight of Gareth and 'Daphne's husband' standing bent double with laughter just a few feet away

Confusion instantly gave way to clarity as it dawned on him that he'd been set up. Gareth came over, still laughing, to confirm what he already knew. I had been Gareth texting and emailing him all along pretending to be Daphne, using a pay as you go phone. The guy he'd enlisted to act the part of Daphne's husband was an old university palwho was an actor.

"I'll get you back for this you bastard, just you wait," Callum told him.

Gareth's lapse into another fit of laughter was his answer.

Saturday morning and Brian arrived at the gym while the others were in the middle of a treadmill session. They were surprised but happy to see him — this despite him appearing like a man who'd just been informed he only had weeks to live. He couldn't face another miserable day staring at the wall and so had dragged himself out for a workout.

Brian stepped onto a vacant treadmill some distance away from the others and started jogging at a slow pace. He only lasted five minutes before he stopped, stepped off and walked away, heading over to the free weight area, where he proceeded to again go through the motions with some perfunctory exercises using half the poundage he normally did.

That he wanted to be left alone was clear and the others did exactly that, purposely working out in another part of the gym.

Later, relaxing in the sauna, the banter unfolded in the usual fashion.

"So, tonight?" Gareth said. "Where to?"

"Tigerlily, where else?" Callum said.

"Not for me, chaps," Gerry announced. "I'm going out for dinner tonight."

"Christ, listen to him," Gareth said. "The first girlfriend he's had in years."

"Jealousy's a terrible thing," Gerry retorted.

"He does have a point, Gareth," Callum opined.

Gareth laughed. "What, me, jealous? You serious?"

"Yes," Gerry and Callum replied in unison.

"Brian," Gareth said, looking for support, "are you listening to this?"

Brian barely looked up. "Not really," he said without enthusiasm.

A short pause ensued, broken by Gareth. "Anyway," he said, "I think it's high time we tried somewhere else."

"Such as?" Callum asked him.

"Oh I don't know. How about the Dome?"

"The Dome?" Callum said. "Have you been in there lately? It's about as empty as your wallet."

"It can't be that empty, surely?" Gerry stepped in sarcastically.

"Ha-ha very funny," Gareth said. "Just because you're all loved up."

"No I'm not," Gerry protested.

"Oh yes you are," Gareth said in an exaggerated voice.

"Yes," Callum said, joining in. "You've met this women and you've abandoned all your mates.

"A sad state of affairs," he continued. "Isn't that right, Brian?"

This time Brian didn't reply. Instead he just raised his eyes from his lap and looked at him. "Gerry abandoning us for a woman," Callum repeated, thinking that Brian mustn't have heard him the first time. "What do you think? Outrageous, isn't it?"

"I don't know," Brian said. "To be honest, I couldn't care less."

And with that he got up and walked out, leaving them to it.

"Never thought I'd see the day," Gareth volunteered with a shake of the head as soon as he'd gone.

Gerry said, "Made the fatal mistake of falling in love and now look at him — finished."

"Look who's talking," Gareth said, winking over at Callum.

Callum, however, was no longer interested in continuing with the banter. Instead, worried about Brian, he got up and followed him out.

"Try and talk some sense into him," said Gareth as he went.

In the changing room, Brian was in his locker removing his shower stuff when Callum appeared. He waited a moment before making his approach.

"Are you okay?"

"I'm fine. Why wouldn't I be?"

Callum watched him for another second or two.

"Listen, if you ever feel like talking about it, I…"

"For the second time, I'm fine," Brian said, cutting him off.

A short awkward silence fell, before Callum said, "Eh, okay, I'll eh…I'll leave you in peace then."

Callum had no sooner started heading back in the direction of the sauna, when Brian stopped what he was doing and said, "I never thought it would happen to me."

Callum turned to face him.

"I can't get her out of my head," Brian went on. "Every minute of every day, she's there.

"Christ, listen to me," he concluded. "I'm pathetic."

"No you're not," Callum said, heading back over to him.

"You found something special is all that happened. Something more important than wondering where to spend a Saturday night looking for who knows what." Brian was somewhat surprised to hear this. "I mean, come on," Callum continued. "You don't really think we're happy, do you?

"All we're doing is putting a brave face on the fact we're so afraid of commitment we're willing to deny ourselves the one thing in life that makes all the shit worth it."

There was a pause as Brian digested Callum's words.

"Thanks."

"No, thank you. You've shown me what I've been missing."

"You've shown all of us."

"Yep, and look how it ended."

"That's where you're wrong," Callum said. "It's still in your hands."

"What do you mean? She's gone. She left."

"She's gone to New York. Last time I checked it's somewhere on this planet."

"What, you think…?"

"I think you should do whatever it takes," Callum told him. Without waiting for a response Callum made his way back to the sauna, leaving Brian with much to contemplate and consider.

## 16

*Fear is excitement without breath*

Waverley train station in the heart of Edinburgh was a daily cornucopia of noise, activity and mayhem — people rushing hither and thither from early morning to last thing at night, accompanied by regular PA announcements on arrivals and departures, while constantly in the background the deep roar of trains arriving and departing — all of it combining with the smell of diesel fumes to mount a relentless assault on the senses.

On this particular morning a heavy downpour merely succeeded in adding to the lugubrious atmosphere. Gerry Scott, however, was immune.

On this Tuesday morning at just after seven he was due on an early train to London to attend a two-day conference on EU criminal law. He was looking forward to escaping his daily routine for the luxury of first class rail travel and a nice hotel. Making the trip even better was the fact he'd just asked Heather to move in with him and she said she would think about it. Mulling over her answer as he made his way to catch the train, confident that she would say yes, had him in such a good mood he almost felt he could float down to London.

The train was waiting on the platform when he got there and quickly locating the First Class section near the front, he jumped on and occupied a table seat, where he took his time getting settled in — first removing his coat and placing it on the overhead rack, then removing his phone, newspaper, book and iPad and placing them on the table, before carefully placing his overnight bag and briefcase alongside his coat on the rack above.

As ever there was an abundance of space in First Class and Gerry sighed with pleasure as he settled into his seat, safe in the knowledge that he would have the entire space to himself for the duration.

By the time the train came to life and began to edge forward, he felt he could sit there all day and luxuriate, accompanied by complimentary cup of coffee after complimentary cup of coffee while wrapped up in thoughts of Heather and how she'd entered his life and transformed it for the better.

When he considered that this time a year ago his life consisted of work, the gym and going out every Saturday night with the guys, he couldn't believe how miserable he'd been while pretending to be happy.

Now, with Heather in his life, he was hitting the gym just three times a week, eating more or less whatever he liked, and hadn't gone near a sunbed in ages. Now he preferred spending his Saturday nights going out to dinner or staying in with a bottle of wine and a movie in Heather's company. And even though workwise things were still shit, thoughts of her helped him get through the day.

In other words, now his daily immersion in the human effluvium at Edinburgh Sheriff Court was just about bearable.

By the time the train pulled into Newcastle, Gerry's thoughts had turned to his plan of visiting M&S branches across central London over the next couple of days.

Since his first and very inauspicious attempt to steal a briefcase from M&S in Princes Street, he'd been on a roll, working his way between the various branches of the store in Edinburgh and Glasgow, taking everything from briefcases, gloves and hats, to coats and jackets. Every returned item netted him a credit voucher, which he used to pay for groceries, thus saving himself a couple of hundred quid a week.

The impulse behind Gerry's Scott's shoplifting was not the money he was saving. It was the buzz of leading a double life and knowing there was more to him than people thought. Of course he would never dream of telling Heather. She wouldn't understand and no doubt would end things immediately. At some point before his luck ran out, he would force himself to stop —just not yet.

As Gerry luxuriated in first class on his way to London, stopping off at his flat back in Edinburgh on his way to the Scottish Parliament at Holyrood was Gareth. And lest the intention of Gareth's visit be misunderstood, no sooner had Heather opened the door to him than they were naked in bed, Gerry's bed, writhing all over one another.

It had been going on for the past couple of weeks, Gareth and Heather meeting on the sly to have it away. The best thing about Heather in bed was her extraordinary talent when it came to fellatio.

The way she went down on Gareth now, running her tongue the length of his shaft, licking his balls, then taking him in her mouth, had him rolling his eyes in ecstasy. He felt his balls contract as they prepared to release his load, but before they did Heather removed him from her mouth and mounted his cock, guiding him into her and sliding up and down, grinding herself all the way down to his balls and up again, until Gareth couldn't have stopped himself coming even if his life depended on it.

Half an hour later they were in the kitchen sipping Gerry's M&S instant coffee from his newly acquired John Lewis coffee mugs. Heather was wearing a short nightshirt and her hair was lying in that just-been-fucked style that Gareth found irresistible.

He put his suit back on, conscious of the fact he had a committee meeting to attend in a little under forty minutes time. But as they sat talking and he drank in the shape of her body under the nightshirt, her bare legs showing, he decided that the meeting could go to hell. Instead he placed his cup down, grabbed her by the hand and led her back in the direction of the bedroom — Gerry's bedroom.

Arriving at the parliament an hour and a half later, having walked there through the unrelenting rain and getting soaked in the process, it was immediately obvious to Gareth that something was wrong. Mary, his PA and researcher, was hardly able to look him in the eye when he walked into the office. When he asked her what the matter was, she barely looked up while limply assuring him thateverything was fine. Moments later, walking along the corridor to get himself a cup of water from the cooler, passing the offices of a few of his fellow Labour MSPs on the way, Gareth felt a distinct chill in the air. Probably to do with my non-appearance at the committee meeting, he automatically assumed. What else could it be? Half an hour later a delegation comprising Iain Macleod and the deputy leader, Gillian Robertson, arrived at his office on an unexpected visit.

Gareth greeted them with a tentative smile. Finally, they were here to offer him a position on the shadow executive. He knew this only because of an email he'd received on the q.t. a couple of weeks ago from one of the girls who worked in central office. She'd been present at the meeting when the post had been discussed and Gareth's name was mentioned.

As the delegation entered it dawned on Gareth that the reason everyone had been so funny with him earlier was down to nothing more than good old fashioned jealousy.

They no doubt already knew that he was about to receive this promotion and resented the fact that here he was, in only his first term as an MSP, being fast tracked to a position within the party leadership. With his guests taking up seats around his desk, the thought of the media profile he would now enjoy brought a smile rather than grimace. With no sinecures in the world of business on the horizon, a career in politics was now his only path and he was determined to walk it to the end.

After exchanging a couple of texts with Heather to let her know that he'd arrived in London, Gerry got settled into his room. The hotel where he was staying was just off Kensington High Street, and after settling in he went over to the conference venue, five minutes walk away, where he checked in and received his accreditation. He then left the venue and made his way down a bustling Kensington High Street in the direction of M&S.

The sky was brilliant blue on a bright and brisk day and the sight of those iconic red buses wending their way along the road, married to the buzz created by so many people of every ethnicity and culture in such close proximity, had his stomach churning with excitement. The Kensington branch of M&S was conveniently located next to the tube station, making this a simple task before jumping straight on the tube to Oxford Street for the next stage of the business at hand.

The first thing Gerry notice upon entering the store via the main entrance was the obvious security presence. Particularly noteworthy here was that the security guards here were young, fit and appeared alert. In contrast, back up the road in Scotland, your typical store security guard appeared unfit, unmotivated and disinterested.

Yet rather than being a reason to be discouraged, the sight of these young up-for-it guys only added to the challenge. With this in mind, stepping on the up-escalator Gerry experienced that familiar rush of adrenalin to which he was now totally addicted.

Reaching menswear on the third floor he browsed for a little bit before arriving at the luggage section. Based on recent experience he knew that returning briefcases without a receipt was no longer the way to go. On the past couple of occasions he'd been given a hard time at customer service; the man or woman behind the counter asking him to wait while they went to check with the manager before processing the return. It was a change in policy that perhaps was a reflection of his success, but which in turn required a fresh approach going forward. Thus, today, Gerry decided that rather than lift a briefcase he would take instead a leather folio case and a pair of leather gloves, items that when carried in his hand would not appear incongruous. The folders were priced at £35 and the leather gloves the same, making a total of £70 for each return.

From Kensington he intended heading to the Oxford Street branch to return said items, then lift the same two items from the menswear department there, return those to the branch at Marble Arch, lift the same items yet again from there, before returning here to Kensington High Street to make his final return of the day. Not a bad day's work, he thought, as he removed a leather folio case from the shelf. Not bad at all.

Before leaving the store, realising he hadn't eaten in hours, he decided to visit the café on the first floor for a quick snack and a latte. In his wallet he had M&S credit vouchers totalling over £500, which meant he was well on top and could look forward to eating for free. Down he went on the escalator, carrying the folio case and leather gloves in his left hand, looking as natural as natural could be and dressed as ever to impress.

He opted for a light brunch consisting of a salad, piece of fruit and a strawberry yogurt. Instead of the latte originally intended, he opted for a black coffee. The strawberry cheesecake looked good but he was able to resist, experiencing that satisfying feeling of being in control as a result.

He took his brunch and settled down at a table against the back wall, affording him a view of the entire café. There he spent a peaceful and thoughtful twenty minutes eating his food and drinking his coffee.

Thereafter he set off for the exit with his items in hand. This entailed descending another level on the escalator to the ground floor. He did so with his inbuilt and by now extremely effective internal radar on full, maintaining a crucial balance between vigilance and insouciance in order to conceal his true purpose.

Hitting the ground floor he had a choice to make between using the main exit or the one over on the far side adjacent to the tube station. A security guard was stationed at both. Gerry spent time browsing while shifting his eyes from one door to the other, reading their respective body language, demeanour, weighing up the state of awareness of each.

The clincher came when the guard at the side exit began a conversation with a female member of staff. In the process his rigid and serious posture evaporated, replaced by that of a young man flirting with a member of the opposite sex.

Gerry's decision was made in that instant. He began a casual walk for the door, keeping sight of the guard in his peripheral vision, ready to stop in an instant if the guy shifted his attention from the girl over to him as he went. The one danger he was unable to control was the possibility that he might be being watched over the store's CCTV. With the security guards in radio contact with whoever was manning the CCTV, this constituted the one and only blind spot of the entire escapade.

Ruminating over the possibility of this being his undoing, he decided that if the worst came to the worst he'd be confident of being able to talk himself out of any situation, no matter how bad. He was a lawyer after all. But as he sauntered on out the door he knew such a desperate measure would not be called for in this instance, as yet again he managed to depart a branch of M&S with goods he hadn't paid for in his possession.

In the tube station, passing through the turnstile on his way down to the platform, he was walking on air. In fact so good did he feel about things he decided to head to Knightsbridge next for a wander round Harrods — not forgetting, of course, the first and the original branch of Harvey Nichols. Reaching the platform he brought out his phone and sent a quick text to Heather.

> *hi sweetheart. me again. just checking in to tell u how much i luv u. kisses, gerry x.*

If only Heather had been able to take a couple of days off work and come down to London, he thought. We would have had a great time. In fact, that's what I'll do as soon as I get back. I'll book us a holiday — take her away somewhere nice. Yes, definitely, what could possibly be better?

And standing there, the sound of the approaching train resounding along the length of the platform, Gerry Scott's heart was filled with gladness.

## 17

*When you come to the end of your rope, tie a knot and hang on*

Brian spent the first half of the flight questioning his sanity. Round and round they went — doubts and the questions that sprung from those doubts — until he found he was unable to sit still and got out of his seat and went for a wander to the end of the aircraft. There by the toilets he spent half an hour engaged in conversation with an old man who'd got up to stretch his legs as well, glad of the temporary respite from his own doom-laden thoughts.

When the flight crew began serving lunch Brian and his new friend ended their conversation and returned to their respective seats. It was only now, eating his lunch and sipping the red wine he'd ordered with his food, that his outlook started to improve and a semblance optimism returned. Ever since Callum put the idea into his head of flying to New York to try and track Tania down, Brian hadn't been able to think about much else, and it was only a day or so after Callum made the suggestion that he booked a flight to depart a week later.

The plan was to stay in New York two weeks with the option of staying longer if needed; Brian having taken a month's sabbatical from his practice with this very goal in mind. Yes, so committed was he to this quest, to finding Tania and winning her back, he was prepared to do anything. For he was now a man that knew exactly what he wanted in life, and nothing, no career or any amount of commitments at home, were going to stand in his way.

As he sat basking in the warm glow of relaxation brought on by his second glass of wine, looking out the window at a blanket of white cloud beneath the wings of the aircraft, thoughts of Tania continued to occupy him.

Who would have thought he would fall head over heels in love again? Just when he was sure he had everything worked out, when he thought that he'd convinced himself he was happy being single, something like this comes along to turn everything upside down.

His thoughts turned to what he would do when he and Tania came face to face again. The realisation he hadn't given this any serious consideration immediately brought back doubts over the wisdom of the entire escapade. What if she still wanted nothing to do with him? What if she freaked out and looked upon him being in New York not as a positive endorsement of his love for her but instead as the deranged actions of a stalker? Christ, Brian thought, if that happens I don't know what I'll do.

But it won't, he thought next, reassuring himself. She loves me, I know she does. I saw it for myself at the airport. That look in her eyes, it told me everything I needed to know. No, she loves me. She does, I just know.

And on that comforting thought he finished the last of the wine in his plastic glass and ordered another.

John F. Kennedy Airport arrivals terminal at just after six in the evening was a scene of chaos — so busy that it took Brian an hour to get through immigration, retrieve his luggage from the baggage carousel, and make his way past customs and on out through the terminal and outside to breathe in his first taste of New York. It was dark and in the distance the lights of Manhattan twinkled like a beacon of everlasting hope. The world may have been plunged into a global recession, but you'd never have guessed it judging by the hustle and bustle of JFK.

First things first, grab a cab.

Over to his right a line of people were standing waiting at the pick-up point for a cab. Every few seconds one pulled up, whereupon the driver would jump out, grab the bags of the next passenger or passengers in line, throw them in the trunk, direct his passengers into the back of the cab, jump back in behind the wheel and speed off. This they did with the efficiency of men for whom every second was money and wasting time was tantamount to a criminal offence.

Brian walked over and took his place at the back of the line. There was a chill October wind blowing in from the Atlantic, but Brian was far too excited to notice or care about anything as trivial as the weather.

His first ever visit to New York and like everyone who arrives for the first time, he was awestruck. Standing in line, shuffling forward every few seconds, he cast his mind back to when he and Gail were trying to decide where to spend their first Christmas together. She wanted to go to New York, while he was partial to a week in the sun somewhere. Back and forth it went, each arguing their case, until finally deciding to conclude the matter with the toss of a coin. Brian won the toss and they ended up in Tenerife on probably the worst holiday they ever had together.

The memory brought a smile as the line continued to move forward, reminding him of a time when he was truly happy and content — when he was in love with Gail, they were about to get married and the future appeared set. Ten minutes later he was sat in the back of a New York cab looking out the window as it ferried him in the direction of Manhattan and the midtown Marriott. His adrenalin was flowing as he thought about seeing Tania, with all doubt and negative thoughts now expunged from his mind. Excitement dictated that he could hardly sit still, and on the back of a sudden urge to strike up a conversation with the cabbie he sat forward and said, "So tell me — how do you like driving a cab in New York? Must be exciting."

The cabbie's eyes shot up to the rearview for a split second before moving back to the road. With a dismissive wave of his left hand, the man replied in an even voice,

"It's not a case of like or dislike. I got five kids at home. They gotta eat."

Brian hadn't been expecting such an abrupt dose of realism in response to the question and sat back, embarrassed at his own naivety.

"You know what I'd like to do," the cabbie went on. "I'd like to get all them Wall Street assholes that fucked up the economy, line 'em up against a wall and shoot the motherfuckers."

"Yes, the economy," Brian uttered weakly, aware of the man's eyes scrutinising him in the rearview. "It's pretty bad here, isn't it?"

"Pretty bad?" the man said, surprised. "Buddy, you obviously been sleepin'. The banks almost went fuckin' bust. People are losing their jobs and their homes left and right in this motherfucker."

"I'm in medicine," Brian said defensively. "It hasn't really affected me."

"It would if you were in medicine over here. People are dropping down dead over this shit. Every time you pick up the paper you read about it. Myself, I got an ulcer the size of a fuckin' cantaloupe."

Once again Brian found himself lost for words.

"Where you from anyhow?" the driver went on. "That an Irish accent?"

"I'm Scottish," Brian corrected him.

"You're from Scotland?"

"Yes."

"So how's it over there with all this shit?"

"Pretty bad. My mind's been on other things."

"Oh yeah? Such as?"

Brian looked out the window. "A woman," he said.

The cabbie shook his head. "I shoulda guessed," he said. "Guy, lemme tell ya somethin' about women. You gotta put your foot in their ass every now then to keep 'em in line. Otherwise they'll walk all over ya and 'fore you know it, you're pussy-whipped.

"You know what I'm sayin'?"

For Brian the conversation was over. "Are we close?" he said with irritation creeping into his voice.

"Not long. Fifteen."

"Good."

Sixteen minutes later the cab pulled up outside the hotel. The volume of pedestrian traffic on the street confirmed that this was a popular part of Manhattan, home to a variety of designer shops, bars and restaurants. By now the light had begun to fade and the temperature had cooled considerably.

Getting out of the cab Brian experienced a fresh surge of excitement. The sheer scale and immensity of the place had already swept him up in its dynamic embrace. The cabbie popped the trunk and got out too. He walked to the rear, reached in the trunk and removed Brian's bags, handing them over to him in exchange for the fare.

"Keep the change," Brian instructed he put forty bucks in the man's hand. A look of obvious and studied disappointment came over the cabbie's face as he looked at it. "What's wrong?" Brian said, wondering if he'd misread the meter. "Doesn't that cover it?"

"You any idea how hard it is to feed six kids in New York?"

"Five kids, I thought you said."

"Five, six, what the fuck difference does it make? Every time I go near this bitch she pops another one."

At the same time as Brian was taking his first tentative steps in New York, in a packed central London, Gerry

Scott emerged from Oxford Street tube station and proceeded to squeeze his way through a tidal wave of humanity along to the Oxford Street branch of M&S. He made his way up to the third floor and over to the customer service desk, where he returned one pair of men's luxury leather gloves and a leather folio case. Taking hold of the £70 credit voucher from the friendly young lady at the counter who processed the return, Gerry took his leave with a hearty farewell.

Descending the escalators to the menswear department on the first floor, he subtly made his way over to the rack where the men's gloves were on display. He selected a pair and then did likewise with a leather folio case. Again, as with the Kensington High Street branch, uniformed security guards were manning every exit and entrance.

Deciding to leave via the back exit he pretended to browse the ladies underwear close to where the security guard there was standing, waiting for his opportunity. Stomach churning, he finally summoned the audacity to do what had to be done and casually sauntered past the guard with the goods in his right hand, price tags suitably concealed, emitting that air of insouciance so crucial to the successful shoplifter.

He continued on down the short set of stairs to the bank of doors that lay just beyond and taking a deep breath, exited the store. Without looking back he turned left and began walking at an even pace along the street, listening for the dreaded sound of running feet coming up from behind. But the sound never came and on he continued, completely unmolested.

Remaining on the side streets running parallel to Oxford Street, he walked all the way along to the main M&S branch at Marble Arch. Here again everything went like clockwork — Gerry first returning the items he'd stolen from the branch at the other end of Oxford Street, collecting his credit voucher, then lifting the same items from the menswear department there, before exiting again.

By now, the time approaching three, he was hungry and exhausted. Deciding therefore to call it a day, he grabbed a cab and headed back to his hotel. On the way he again texted Heather to tell her he loved her, deciding as he did to use the accumulated M&S vouchers to get her something nice while down here.

At the same time Gerry was sitting in the back of a black cab wending its way through the chaotic streets of central London, Gareth Cairns was sitting the office of the presiding officer of the Scottish Parliament.

The delegation that had come to visit him earlier—made up party leader Iain Macleod, his deputy Gillian Robertson, and later joined by the party's chief whip, Ahmed Khan — had not come to offer him the promotion he'd initially assumed. Oh no, instead they'd arrived to break the news that evidence had emerged implicating him in a corruption scandal, one involving a prominent local businessman paying a substantial sum to ensure he received planning permission for a hotel development in Gareth's constituency of Edinburgh Central; Gareth having falsely assured the man that he had the requisite contacts at the council with this in mind.

The businessman in question decided to approach the party's leadership when the planning permission failed to materialise and Gareth ignored his demands for the return of the fee for services un-rendered, threatening to go to the press if something wasn't done about it. In support of his threat he provided evidence in the form of text messages, emails and a record of a bank transfer to an account in Jersey.

Having listened to Macleod present the evidence of his misdeeds, Gareth took a moment to comport himself. "Okay, what do you want me to do?" he said quietly.

"Well," Macleod began solemnly, "by rights this should be the subject of a parliamentary inquiry. It should also be the subject of a criminal investigation by the police." Macleod paused for effect. "However, after giving it careful thought, we've decided that such an outcome would do immeasurable damage to the parliament's reputation.

"We've decided therefore to give you the opportunity of making this go away quietly, with the minimum of fuss." Gareth looked at Macleod, then at Gillian Robertson beside him, a charge of electricity passing through him at the get-out-of-jail card it appeared he was being handed.

"How?" he asked in a tremulous voice, one befitting a man whose fate was no longer his to control.

"Return the money in full within forty-eight hours and resign your seat with immediate effect."

"You can cite a family illness as your reason for resigning," Robertson chimed in. "Given that you don't hold any office bearing position within the party or parliament, there shouldn't be too many questions," she added.

"The alternative, as I say," Ian MacLeod said, "is a full parliamentary inquiry followed by the strong possibility of a police investigation, bringing with it the near certainty of a criminal prosecution.

"The choice is yours."

Gareth sat there like a pillar of salt, wondering where it all went wrong? Had his father been right when, all those years ago, he'd called him a "waste of space.?"

Had he?

## 18

*It couldn't have happened anywhere but in little old New York*

Waking just before nine after a peaceful and rejuvenating first night's sleep in New York, doubts about what he was doing made an unwelcome return to Brian's consciousness. What now? He thought ruefully. How the hell will I go about finding her? All I know is that she works for a bank on Wall Street. I don't even know which one. The topic of work and careers hardly came up during our time together.

Before departing Edinburgh, Brian had spent an evening on the computer trying to track her down via Google. Tania Gonzalez was her name, she told him, and he duly typed it into his browser. Inexplicably, nothing came up. Surely if she's a Wall Street executive something should come up, he thought as he sat there staring at the screen blankly.

It was later that evening, having abandoned the attempt and relaxing with some Chardonnay, that the possibility that she may still be using her married name at work occurred to him. Either that or Gonzalez was her married name and she used her maiden name at work.

Thinking about this now as he lay in bed surveying in detail his hotel room for the first time, it came to him that all he knew about this woman had come in that short emotional exchange at the airport when she'd divulged the loss of her baby and the fact her husband left her over it.

This was all he really knew about her and the realisation depressed him, hitting him like a hard fist with the cold truth that he'd jumped on a flight and travelled halfway across the world in pursuit of a woman he'd spent just a few weeks with. Infatuation, that's what this was, nothing more. How could it be anything else? Love? What is love if not an addiction to another human being? Hadn't he come to this conclusion way before now? And hadn't he vowed never to allow himself to succumb to it again?

Throwing the duvet back, Brian got up and walked into the en-suite for his morning piss. He then stepped into the shower and spent ten minutes under a jet of piping hot water, reminding him of the time when he and Tania had showered together at his flat.

The memory aroused him and he stepped out of the shower with an erection. Ignoring it, he dried himself with one of the hotel's large white fluffy towels before brushing his teeth, applying deodorant, massaging some moisturiser into his face, then fixing his hair. Back in the room he switched on the TV to watch the news as he got himself dressed.

The unfamiliar sight and sounds of American television provided the background noise as he went over to the closet and brought out an ensemble that consisted of a pair of jeans, shirt and v-neck sweater. By the time he finished getting dressed, he was looking forward to breakfast. Before heading out, though, he stopped to watch the news for a moment, reporting the loss of more jobs and more bad news vis-a-vis the stock market.

 It was time to make a move and, grabbing his jacket, wallet and phone, off he went. The hotel offered a fully catered complimentary breakfast for guests, but Brian was keen to get out of the hotel and find a place to eat somewhere nearby and plan his movements for the rest of the day. The noise of traffic combined with the din of countless conversations among the sea of pedestrians on the street to create a wall of noise that set the blood flowing through his veins.

 Time was the commodity that best defined New York and everywhere he looked people were rushing back and forth with a demeanour of God-help-anyone who dares get in my way. On the opposite corner across the street was a deli. Deciding to head there for breakfast, Brian joined a small group of people standing on the corner waiting for the lights to change.

The deli was busy with a constant traffic of people entering and exiting with their orders. The seating area was near empty, no doubt because at this hour during the week people were in a hurry to get to work and didn't have time to sit and relax over breakfast. Brian joined the line at the counter waiting to be served.

Doing the serving were two young pugnacious looking Italian dudes, barking out invitations to order before making said orders up with practiced speed and dexterity. The effect of this no-nonsense dynamic on Brian was to compel him to quickly scan the menu on the board above the counter to ensure that when his turn came to order he didn't embarrass himself by hesitating. His concern in this regard was proved correct when the guy standing two places in front in the line stepped forward to give his order.

"Yo!" barked one of the Italians.

In response the guy, his deep tan and bleached blonde hair striking an incongruous note, pointed to the menu board. "How many calories are in the tofu?"

"Fuck you, I'm serving somebody else," the guy behind the counter immediately came back before doing exactly that, letting everyone know in the process that in this establishment you don't fuck around asking stupid questions.

Five minutes later Brian was sitting at a table by the window, tucking into a ham and cheese bagel and some black coffee. Washing over him was that sense of anticipation you experience when you first arrive in a new city, especially one as big and dynamic and with as much history as New York.

Caught up in the optimism that rode in on the back of this feeling, Brian began to convince himself that locating Tania and winning her back was going to be a straightforward exercise. He'd even begun to visualise the surprise on her face when she saw him prior to running into his arms. As he continued to eat his bagel and drink his coffee, a smile appeared on his face at the thought. I *am* going to find her and we *are* going to be together — yes.

After finishing his breakfast, he made his way to the nearest subway station according to the directions he'd been given by one of the Italians behind the counter. Outside, hang a right, the guy had told him, walk two blocks along Amsterdam, then hang another right and go another block along. Subway's on the corner.

Swept along in the sea of pedestrian traffic, Brian duly arrived at the subway while struggling manfully to maintain the pretence of belonging. Everyone here moved with a purpose to leave him feeling more self conscious and hesitant than he would've felt otherwise. Purchasing his ticket at the booth inside the station, he made his way through the turnstile and arrived at the platform. There, a black guy was walking up and down singing the Marvin Gaye classic 'I Heard It Through The Grapevine'. That he was making as good a job of it as old Marvin ever did himself was clearly lost on the majority of those standing on the crowded platform waiting for the train, however, reflected in the poor guy going almost completely ignored.

Two hours later, Brian got off the train at Wall Street, having transferred to the Lexington Avenue Line at Times Square, where he'd taken the opportunity to stop off and peruse a few of the sights, purposely wasting a couple of hours so as to get to Wall Street just in time for the start of the lunchtime rush. He passed at Times Square watching a man playing the bagpipes, before moving on to a group of men and women espousing a doomsday scenario involving the end of white Christian civilisation.

Bored with this after a while, he moved on to one of the many coffee shops that were dotted around. There he sat browsing a newspaper in the company of a tuna salad, Italian bread, and a diet coke. Times Square during the day was a disappointment, he decided, packed with tourists, gaudy neon signs and dodgy looking shops selling cheap computers and other electrical goods.

Later, emerging from Wall Street subway station up the stairs to the street, he was met by the sight of the world's financial capital in all its architectural splendour. He stepped to the side and stood taking it all in for a few minutes while working out his next move. The time was approaching midday and the streets would soon be awash.

For lack of a better idea, Brian set off on a slow walk down the street, hoping somehow, some way, that by dint of sheer luck he might catch sight of Tania. The sidewalk full by the time he was a quarter of the way down, he tingled with excitement at the knowledge that at that precise moment she was in one of the grand buildings that lined both sides of the street. Either that or she was out on the street itself.

By the time he was halfway down Wall Street the need for another caffeine fix prompted him to stop off at a little coffee booth, where he ordered a latte. It was the perfect spot from which to stand and watch the world go by, which he did in awe at the sheer dynamism of the place. No wonder New York is commonly referred to as the capital of the world.

Then, out of nowhere, a woman walked passed him from behind with long dark hair and a familiar gait. Tania? Is that her? With his heart instantly set thumping at the prospect, Brian began following, as with every step he grew more convinced he'd found her.

"Tania," he called out, adrenalin pumping as he upped the pace and started jogging to close the distance. "Tania?" He drew closer until, with her just six feet away from him, she walked into the arms of a man standing outside a restaurant. The man she was with looked at Brian over her shoulder.

"Hey man, you got a problem?"

The woman in his arms turned to look. It wasn't Tania and Brian quickly walked on, face burning with embarrassment and disappointment as the couple turned and made their way into the restaurant. If only he knew that inside that very restaurant at that very moment, Tania was eating lunch in the company of her friend Lucy.

"Anyway," Lucy said, continuing their conversation, "Greg says we need to think about moving closer to Kyle so we can be on hand to give him the support he needs."

"But Kyle's at Harvard," Tania said. "That's in Boston."

"That's what I told him," Lucy replied, "but he won't listen. He says we need to be close to make sure Kyle succeeds."

"Honey, you can't move to Boston. What about your career?"

"I told him that too."

"Plus," Tania went on, "Kyle isn't going to appreciate having his parents camped outside the university. He's not a kid anymore. He needs to grow, find his own path."

Lucy sighed. "It's so fucking depressing. Every time I think about it I get stomach ache."

"Lucy, the problem here isn't Kyle. The problem is Greg and his inability to let go. What's got into him recently?"

"Oh I don't know. Midlife crisis, I guess." Lucy swallowed a mouthful of salad, washed it down with a sip of water and went on, "Last weekend I caught him sitting at the front window with his camera filming the neighbour's dog."

"In God's name, why?"

"He said he was trying to catch it doing a shit in the garden so he can sue the owner."

Tania put her fork down. "Okay, that's it, I need to talk to him."

"I wish you would," Lucy said. "He's driving me crazy."

"Let's arrange dinner at your place next week. Sounds to me like all he needs is a good old fashioned foot in the ass — metaphorically speaking, of course."

"Screw metaphorically," Lucy said, both of them laughing at the thought. Then Lucy said, "Why don't you bring your new date along?"

Tania's facial expression revealed her lack of enthusiasm at the idea. "What's wrong?" Lucy inquired.

"Nothing."

"Things didn't work out?"

Tania sighed. "I don't know."

"But I thought you said he was gorgeous?"

"He is," Tania said. "He's also the most boring man on the planet. Over dinner last week he spent two hours talking about his portfolio."

"What is it with men nowadays?" Lucy cut in. "They're all such insecure assholes."

"I'm supposed to be meeting him for dinner again this week. I'm thinking of cancelling."

"No, you should go," Lucy said, "First dates are always difficult. A second date and you know for sure."

Tania took a moment to ponder her friend's advice. By now the restaurant was packed. Lucy looked up and saw a couple of work colleagues at an adjacent table and gave them a perfunctory greeting, before turning her attention back to Tania and the matter at hand.

"You wanna know what I really think though?"

Tania looked at her, waiting for the rest.

"You haven't been the same since you got back from Scotland. I think you're still pining for this guy you met there."

"No, that was just a fling," Tania replied with a dismissive wave of the hand; her reply a little took quick and her gesture a little too contrived to be fully convincing. "I don't believe you."

"Come on, stop that."

"No-no, you can't fool me, "Lucy went on. "I know you. You really fell for this guy. Admit it. He got to you. Didn't he?"

Tania was almost tempted to agree. But do that and she risked opening a Pandora's Box of regret that she could well do without.

So instead she smiled and said, "It's in the past." Next, she checked her watch. "Shoot, I gotta go. I've got a meeting with my boss tomorrow and I need to prepare a report."

Tania got up from the table, gesturing the waiter over to get her coat.

"I thought you were okay until two?"

"That was before he requested this meeting. We're having problems with one of our Latin American accounts. I'm guessing as usual it'll be yours truly who's going to have to deal.

"You stay and finish your food," she continued. "I'll get the check on the way out."

Before Lucy got a chance to say reply, Tania kissed her on the cheek and started for the door.

A minute later she came out of the restaurant straight into a heavy downpour that had people scurrying for shelter. Without an umbrella, Tania did likewise, running in the direction of her office while holding the collar of her expensive coat up around her neck in a futile attempt to shield her from the rain.

Three doors along from the restaurant was Franco's Coffee Shop, one of the more popular destinations for lunch in and around Wall Street. Tania usually decamped here for lunch at least once a week, but today she rushed past. As she did Brian took another sip of his wine at his seat by the window, having momentarily averted his eyes from the street to look at the couple at the table over to his right. They were looking at one another like two people blissfully in love and the sight left him sad. The sound of the rain battering off the window behind him was the perfect sound effect to a mood oscillating between melancholy and futility. The vibration of an incoming text on his phone distracted him. He brought it out of his inside pocket and read the message. It was from Callum.

> *Hi m8, just checking in. Hope it's going well over there. If you fancy a chat, give me a shout. Cheers.*

Brian began to type his reply, but then decided against it and put the phone back in his pocket. He took another sip of his wine. The couple he'd been watching had finished their lunch and were making their way out.

## 19

*Life is but a walking shadow*

After pinging Brian a text Callum placed his phone back down on the table and looked over at Gareth, who'd just placed a forkful of salmon and watercress into his mouth, preparatory to washing it down with mineral water. Like Callum, Gareth was eager to find out how Brian was getting on in New York and the two of them were looking forward to his response.

"This place is dead," Callum opined, casting his eyes around the restaurant and bar of Harvey Nichols.

"It's never that busy during the week," Gareth said.

"It usually is on a Friday though."

"There's a recession on, remember?"

"I think people are going over the score about this bloody recession," Callum said. "It's all you ever hear now — recession, credit crunch, the world is nigh. If you ask me, it's all in the mind — like some kind of self-fulfilling prophecy. There's nothing wrong with the economy that won't correct itself in a few months."

"I really hope you're right."

"I'm serious," Callum pressed. "This bloody recession's been hyped to the point where it's taken on the character of a religion."

Gareth was still eating his salad, ravenous after their workout earlier.

"Yes, I agree" he said, wiping his mouth with his napkin. "People are enjoying wallowing in the misery of it all. It's almost like a drug with some people."

"A misery drug," Callum said, thinking out loud. "That's the perfect way to describe it."

Gareth sat there doing his best to maintain a positive front. He was yet to reveal that he'd been forced to resign as an MSP. In truth, he was still struggling to process everything that had happened a week on from his meeting in Iain Macleod's office.

Previously, he'd been able to fall back on his father's influence and connections, which in this kind of situation would simply mean picking up the phone and getting fixed up with something else.

Not anymore.

His father was seriously ill, stricken with cancer, and Gareth daren't risk tipping him or his mother over the age by revealing news of his inglorious demise. Saying that, though he questioned himself for thinking along such lines, his father's own demise brought with it the promise of a nice inheritance, so all was not lost.

As for Callum, ever since his clear-the-air meeting with his new bank manager a few weeks ago, a meeting that ended to his great relief with the news that his personal overdraft and credit facility would remain as they were, he'd been riding the proverbial crest. Yes, the country was in the midst of a deep recession. And, yes, the property market, once a gold mine in Edinburgh, was currently flat on its arse. No matter, Callum was convinced that give it six months and things will have turned around and his various developments would be back up and running. Buoyed by this glass half-full outlook, he'd never felt more relaxed.

"Still no reply from Brian, I see," Gareth volunteered.

"I know," Callum said. "I hope everything's all right."

Pierre appeared at the table. "Everything good, gentleman? More champagne?"

"Yes, another bottle please," Callum said. "Put it on my account."

"Oh, you have a friend there," Pierre said, winking at Gareth.

Changing the subject, Callum wiped his mouth with his napkin. "Pierre, you're a man of the world. Let me ask you a question."

"Nine inches."

Laughter.

"No, seriously," Callum went on, "Gareth and I were having a discussion about New York earlier — analysing its current status and importance within the fashion industry. What's your take on it? Do you agree with me that New York has overtaken Milan and Paris?"

"This has something to do with Brian, yes?"

"Kinda-sorta," Gareth said. "Brian's over there right now, and it got us thinking about the place."

"I see," Pierre said, before pausing to consider the question with the seriousness it deserved. "New York," he said, "is in my opinion now equal to Paris and Milan in its importance within the fashion industry. The size of the US market and the significant media presence are significant factors.

However, the fashion industry still needs to remain based in Europe. Here it is closer to textile suppliers and manufacturers in Asia, for example, and the European market continues to expand, especially with the emergence of Russia as a major consumer of high end fashion in recent years."

"Pierre, I've said it before and I'll say it again," Gareth declared. "You're a genius."

"I'll toast to that," Callum declared, picking up his champagne. Gareth did likewise and they clinked glasses and took a drink.

"How's Brian?" Pierre inquired. "Have you heard from him?"

"I just sent him a text. He hasn't replied."

"He's been gone a few days now, yes?"

"Three days," Gareth said.

"He's in love," Callum said.

"He has, how you say, lost it?" Pierre said, in response to which the guys smiled appropriately.

"Okay," Pierre went on, "I have to get back to work. Another bottle of champagne coming up."

Pierre left behind him a sombre and reflective atmosphere at the table. All of a sudden the mood had changed. "Well," Callum said, breaking the silence.

"Where to this weekend? Tigerlily?"

"Where else?"

"I'll give Gerry a shout, see what he's up to. Like Brian, I think he's in love. There must be something the air."

Gareth looked down at his napkin, wracked with guilt over the fact he'd been banging Heather on a regular basis.

Callum said, "I wonder how he's getting on in London at his conference? He's probably in Harrods shopping as we speak."

"Probably is," Gareth said, thinking about Heather in bed. "He probably is."

## 20

*The only sin is getting caught*

The office was smaller than Gerry had imagined. It consisted of two rooms: the first containing nothing apart from a bare wooden table around which three hard plastic chairs were arrayed: the second even smaller, containing a bank of monitors which at that moment were being manned by an overweight woman in uniform. She was sitting in front of them studying the footage being beamed back to her from security cameras covering the entire store.

Gerry was sitting in a plastic chair on one side of the desk, facing the door. One of the store detectives who'd apprehended him was sitting opposite filling out a form, while the other was standing just inside the door, following the usual procedure designed to block any attempt at escape, however unlikely.

Both were in plain clothes, though going by their appearance and demeanour it would not have taken a genius to pick them out. That Gerry failed to was indicative of complacency having set in— a fatal flaw in the armoury of any self-respecting shoplifter.

Sauntering back into the Kensington branch of M&S, he'd taken himself straight up to menswear and there picked up a leather briefcase and a pair of luxury leather gloves before heading back down to the ground floor and for the exit without stopping for a second to ensure he hadn't attracted any unwanted attention, head filled with thoughts of Heather and calling her as soon as he got back to the hotel.

Reaching the exit, the store detectives appeared in front of him as if from nowhere. The fright Gerry received at their sudden presence paralysed him to the point where he failed to utter a word while being escorted back inside. As they approached the back office, the fog of shock in which his brain was enveloped began to dissipate as he began to weigh up the gravity of the situation.

Even so, sitting at the table in this bare security office, he still refused to acknowledge that his life was about to undergo a fundamental change. On the contrary, Gerry was in a strangely euphoric mood, even attempting to engage the store detectives in conversation.

The store detectives were happy to oblige him, especially as people like him, well dressed and articulate, were not the type they were used to dealing with. Usually this office was host to assorted drug addicts, alcoholics and neds whose appearance drew attention as soon as they walked into the store. It was rare they encountered someone like Gerry, and whenever they did it never failed to intrigue them.

"So how did you guys catch me out?" Gerry said, feeling comfortable enough to provide them with a tacit admission of guilt to confirm his status as a rank amateur. A successful shoplifting conviction largely revolved around the issue of intent. For someone to admit that they had come into the store intending to steal was crucial in securing a conviction, especially as the courts usually gave people like this particular suspect the benefit of the doubt otherwise. The store detective standing by the door revealed that they'd watched him walk out of the store earlier that morning with goods he hadn't paid for and that when he returned they had his image on file. The guy, Mohammad Kaballo his name was, went on to ask Gerry if he'd been to any other stores around central London that day, hoping to get him to open up and thereby build a stronger case.

As soon as he asked the question, Gerry's brain switched gear and instantly his mood changed. Like a man receiving a electric shock, he realised for the first time the true nature of the predicament he was in and what the actual consequences could be. What would it mean for his career? More importantly, how would it affect his relationship with Heather if she found out?

Before he could answer either question a sharp knock on the door heralded the arrival of the police. As they walked in, Gerry's heart sank like a stone landing on water.

As Gerry Scott was being escorted out of the Kensington branch of M&S in London in handcuffs, Brian was watching the news in his hotel room in mid-Manhattan. He was bored and he was lonely having just got off the phone with Gail, upin calling home to find out how the kids were doing.

This, at least, was the excuse.

The truth is that he wanted to hear Gail's voice in response to the arrival of memories of their time together while flipping channels in his room. As he did he found himself asking why he decided to leave the marriage? Had it been that bad? Was life as a single man really better than when he was with Gail and the kids?

The stark and growing realisation he was forced to confront was that he'd made a mistake and that life in the just over two years he'd been single had not been better at all. For a period, yes, he'd enjoyed the freedom of being able to sleep with whoever he wanted whenever he wanted. Refocusing his priorities and putting himself first had likewise been a change he'd enjoyed initially; going to the gym with the guys, shopping, having his own space, being able to come home to peace and quiet instead of the demands of a young family, it had all been great for a spell. Making things easier was the way he and Gail had remained close despite being apart.

The absence of acrimony and bitterness almost succeeded in convincing him that they weren't separated, merely involved in an open relationship. They even continued to sleep together now and then after splitting up, only stopping when Gail met Graham. Strange, but Brian had never felt jealous over Gail's relationship with Graham. For one thing he had no right to be — not when he was bedding different women on a regular basis. More than that he wanted to see her happy. And with Graham, arsehole though he might be, she seemed genuinely content.

Perhaps, though, he was guilty of looking back on their relationship through rose tinted glasses. Maybe the reason he wanted to talk to Gail was because of his feelings for Tania; this woman who'd arrived in his life out of nowhere and whom he hadn't been able to get out of his mind since.

He had lost count of the number of times he'd relived their exchange at Edinburgh Airport, where he'd made a desperate attempt to get her to change her mind about leaving.

The pain on her face when she'd blurted out the stuff about losing her baby and the ensuing breakdown of her marriage left him speechless, he recalled. Looking back on it now he was convinced it was in the five-seconds of silence that elapsed after she'd shared this with him that he lost her.

If only I'd been able to find the words to reassure her. If only….No, stop. All you're doing is torturing yourself. Don't do it.

But he couldn't help himself; the memory of the airport exchange just wouldn't go away and he'd lost count of the number of times he'd replayed it in his mind. It was — it was those five critical seconds of silence that were responsible for his decision to jump on a plane and come over here to try and find her.

All he wanted was another chance, an opportunity to see if he could turn things round. Maybe it's guilt over his inability to reach out precisely when she needed him to. Her face, he'll never forget, revealed a woman who was vulnerable and scared and desperate for someone to come into her life and protect her. The thought of her out there alone without him was horrible. I wonder what she's doing now, he thought as he again began aimlessly flipping channels. I wonder if she thinks about me as much as I think about her.

Just three miles away on the Upper Eastside, Tania was seated across from Mike in Luigi's, an Italian restaurant they'd come to on his recommendation. They were halfway through the main course, which for him consisted of lasagne and for her spaghetti carbonara. The food and the wine were less than impressive, and the choice of restaurant questionable. Taking her friend Lucy's advice, she'd decided to give Mike another chance with a second date. It was a decision she'd already begun to regret.

"So, as I was saying, the energy market has bottomed out and I'm thinking of using my real estate portfolio as collateral to borrow and invest heavily in order to take advantage."

Mike stopped to refill his wine glass from the bottle on the table. After doing so he placed the bottle back without, Tania noticed, offering to top her up as well.

"I was in Scotland recently," she said. "Have you ever been to Europe?"

"I've hardly been out of New York," he said, before forking more lasagne into his mouth. "Why go see the world when the world is right here? If I'm going to make money there's no better place than the US. I mean, do you have any idea how much money Wall Street generates each year? We're talking more than the combined GDP of the entire African continent."

Tania smiled and returned to the food on her plate. However she'd lost her appetite and settled for pushing it around on the plate with her fork.

"Oh, that reminds me," Mike went on. "If you ever come across a hot investment tip at work, be sure to let me know. There's a commission in it if it holds up."

Tania nodded, smiled, and took another sip of wine. She did so cursing Lucy, making a silent vow never to trust her advice again. Then she thought about Brian for the umpteenth time that day, wishing against her better judgement that she could turn back time.

## 21

*When I let go of what I am, I become what I might be*

It was two nights later, at just after ten past eight, when Brian finally admitted defeat. His notion of somehow tracking Tania down and the two of them reuniting in a passionate embrace had given way to the unvarnished truth that he'd only been deluding himself. More than that, over the past five days of catching the subway to Wall Street every morning and wandering up and down expecting to run into her, he'd begun to pine for his kids. It had been over a week since he'd seen them last and yesterday, when he called to find out how they were, Gail put them on the phone and they both started crying, asking where he was and why they couldn't see him.

Listening to them crying almost reduced Bian to tears too, and coming off the phone he was consumed with self-recrimination. What kind of man are you? How could you be so selfish as to leave your kids to fly halfway across the world to chase some woman you hardly even know? Have your actually lost your mind?

Taking stock of all this while eating dinner alone in the hotel, he put his fork down, wiped his mouth with the napkin on his lap, got his phone out and called the airline to reschedule his departure for the following day.

Half an hour later, having booked his seat on a 4pm flight, Brian left the hotel for some air and spent the next couple of hours walking the streets of Manhattan with no destination in mind.

As he walked he made a conscious effort to take it all in — the sounds and sights of a city renowned the world over as the beating heart of the industrialised world. He wandered down to Times Square, curious to see how it looked at night when bathed in neon. Gaudy and vulgar were the words that inmediately came to mind when he got there; his senses assaulted by a gargantuan display of the excess that defined Western civilisation. Is this it, he asked himself while looking up at a massive neon ad for a major electronics company? It this really how far we've progressed?

Like Leicester Square and Piccadilly Circus in London, Times Square in New York was a tourist magnet. Even late at night the place was awash with camera-clicking hordes of them getting their fix.

Brian didn't linger and continued south along Seventh Avenue towards downtown. His disappointment at the thought of returning home without Tania, without even managing to see her, was offset by the prospect of seeing his kids again. It was hard for him to admit that he'd taken them for granted over these last couple of years, but take them for granted he had.

Yes, he'd continued to spend his couple of days a week with them, but being honest with himself he had done so more out of a sense of duty and obligation than anything else. Over the two months in which he'd lost himself with Tania, they'd hardly entered into his thoughts at all. It was only when Harry was rushed into hospital that he was reminded that first and foremost he was a dad with responsibilities and people who depended on him. Tania's reaction when she found out he had children had shamefully led to him regretting the fact. And though it had only been a fleeting regret, it was still a source of shame.

As he continued walking down Seventh Avenue, skyscrapers looming up on either side like sentinels in the dark, he was in the throes of an inner conflict. He might be single, but more important was that there were two young children who needed him and whom he needed in turn. How to reconcile the two was something he had never considered up until now. Could they be reconciled? Wouldit have been possible to satisfy the demands of both if he'd managed to find Tania and they began a serious relationship?

There were more questions than answers and rather than allow himself to spend his last night in New York in turmoil, he decided to return to the hotel for an early night and accept that there were just some things in life outwith man's control. He and Tania just weren't meant to be together and the time had come to let it go.

Early the next morning and Wall Street was its usual tableau of chaos, with people pouring out of the subway station and headed for another day of relentless toil in one of the huge offices that colonised this world-famous street that was home to the world's major banks and financial institutions. Billions of dollars were generated here each day and billions were lost. The global economic crisis that had plunged the world into the worst recession since the 1930s started in this small corner of the planet, spreading out to engulf billions of people around the world like a great crashing tidal wave of despair and ruin.

Unfettered greed, this was Wall Street's *raison d'être*, but only in the bad times did people complain. When the going was good they rode the wave, delighted to reap the opportunities afforded by the ability to borrow money right and left with very few if any questions asked. Need a loan to buy a house? No problem, it's yours. Even if you can't afford the repayments, take it anyway and we'll worry about the repayments later. Money for a new car, business loan, home improvements? It's right here whenever you want it. All you have to do is pick up the phone and the money will be wired to your account in no time.

Derivatives trading, subprime lending, hedge funds, credit default swaps, securities — the language of unfettered greed codified and deified in, this, the world's financial capital. And even though now the very words Wall Street may have left a bitter taste in the mouths of millions of ordinary Americans and people across the world, Wall Street didn't care. Here the only thing that mattered was the next deal and more commission.

Tania was late. When she arrived at the office, coming out of the elevator like a woman on a mission, she passed Mary her PA with nothing to say except, "Shit!"

Mary got up from her desk and followed her into her office. "I told him you were held up on the subway," she said. "Is everything okay?"

"I was up all night preparing this damn report and I overslept," Tania said, dumping her coat before removing the relevant file from her briefcase. "So, no, everything is not okay."

"Coffee?"

"Don't have time," Tania replied while marching out of the office again clutching the file containing her report.

"Wish me luck."

"Good luck," Emily called back just before Tania had moved out of earshot.

Charles Browder had been the bank's vice chairman for five years and in that time had promoted Tania twice. When she was promoted to Head of International Accounts it was felt within the bank that she was being groomed for a seat on the board within the next few years. The performance of her department under her tutelage had been exemplary; only in post eight months she had succeeded in turning things around after the huge losses incurred as a consequence of the financial crisis. This was largely attributable to Tania's sound judgment in ensuring that existing international investors and customers were reassured as to the banks ability to weather the storm. As such it was always a warm smile that greeted her whenever she entered her Browder's office.

But not on this morning. This morning was different.

Instead, entering his office after the usual perfunctory knock, Tania instantly absorbed the pained expression on her Charles Browder's face as he invited her to take a seat. More significant still was the presence of Rob Taylor, son of the bank's CEO who'd recently been promoted to a seat on the board, thus demonstrating that on Wall Street nepotism was alive and kicking.

"Hi," Tania said as she took her seat, Taylor's eyes studying her and making her uncomfortable as she did. "Sorry I'm late."

"Don't worry about it," Browder said, before averting his eyes to the file that was in front of him on his desk. In the brief silence that followed Tania and Rob Taylor exchanged a look of mutual dislike. This she realised was not going to be pleasant, not with this asshole present. Something was wrong.

"So," Tania said to her boss, eager to get things started, "you requested a meeting."

"Yes," Browder replied, still looking down at the file in front of him. "Yes, I did." When he finally raised his eyes he could hardly bring himself to look Tania in the eye. "Look, I…" Browder said before pausing. "I just want you to know that your performance since taking on your new role has been first class."

"But?"

Browder let out a sigh. "But as you are aware the economy has taken a hit and…well…"

"You're fired," Taylor announced.

"I'm sorry, Tania," Browder said weakly. "I tried. I really tried. However the board feels…"

"Your department's being wound up and merged with mine," Taylor interjected again, smiling.     Tania hadn't been expecting this, not in a million years, and all at once found herself struggling to keep her composure as tears started to well up behind her eyes.

"Is this true?" she said, looking at her boss.

Browder's silence was her answer.

"I don't understand," she said. "My department is the only one in this entire organisation that's on course to meet its targets this year."

"Yes," Taylor said, "but unfortunately some of our major shareholders aren't too happy with the figures and the board has decided that some of the fat needs to be trimmed.

"No offence meant, of course."

"Oh really?" Tania shot right back. "And does the board know that its newest addition regularly hits the bathroom to top up on cocaine."

"You bitch," Taylor sneered. "You fucking bitch. Fuck you."

"You already tried to. Or have you forgotten that night at the Bistro when you were so fucked up on coke you couldn't see straight?"

Taylor's face flushed red with anger and humiliation combined. Listening in, Browder could do nothing except put his head in his hands and wish for the day to end.

"If you don't mind," Tania said, "I'd really like to get out of here."

Browder nodded his assent and in response Tania got up and headed for the door.

"Oh, and just so you know," she said to Taylor. "Word round the campfire is that your dick is so small you need a magnifying glass just to take a piss.

"No offence meant."

She arrived back at her office fifteen minutes later via the bathroom, where she'd occupied a cubicle and cried at the news that her world had just been turned upside down. Mary knew right away that something was wrong. After waiting five minutes, she got up and tentatively walked through to find out what. Tania was in the midst of boxing up her belongings when she got there.

"Yep, it's exactly what it looks like," Tania said, placing pictures of her parents into the box along with various other bits and pieces. Before Mary could find the words to articulate her shock, two security guards arrived to escort her boss out of the building.

The entire office came to a standstill as Tania Gonzalez walked to the elevators carrying her box, a security guard on either side. Determined not to crack, Tania kept her eyes fixed straight ahead, studiously avoiding any eye contact with her colleagues, many of whom she'd known for years.

By the time she finally emerged from the building onto the street, her legs were shaking and she felt nauseous. Fortunately the fresh air hit her like an elixir and she was able to regroup and carry on, striding along Wall Street with her box, which in this part of the world meant one thing and one thing only.

She'd been fired.

Half an hour later, Brian was sitting in the back of a yellow cab on his way to the airport. He was in a reflective mood, thinking about Tania and what might have been. Tania was thinking about Brian at the exact same moment. On the subway heading uptown, the box containing her things was sitting on her lap as she relived the last time she saw him at the airport back in Edinburgh. Her initial conclusion on the flight home had been that their time together had been nothing more than a fling. But as the days and weeks passed — during which she found she couldn't stop thinking about him — she began to feel that it had been more than that. Time and again she'd been tempted to try to get in touch to see if he felt the same. But then the pain of knowing that if she did she would be forcing him to choose between her and his kids, knowing that regardless of how much she wanted to be with him she wouldn't be willing to move to Scotland, always stayed her hand.

Perhaps the lesson to be drawn from what she was feeling was that she was ready to meet someone and be happy again. In coming into her life and showing her there more important things than a career, Brian had done more than he could ever possibly know. The pain of the break up of her marriage had gone, she'd spent the necessary time required to process it all, and it was time to be whole again. At that moment, as the subway train continued on its journey uptown Tania actually experienced a surge of excitement at what the future might hold. Didn't a wise man once say that every exit is an entrance?

Having finally reached the departures lounge at JFK, Brian was experiencing his own sense of optimism and hope as he watched a couple of kids around the same age as his own playing with their parents. In a world in the grip of a recession the one thing capable of providing any sense of hope for the future, he'd come round to believing, was the love of a family. Previously he'd been cynical in this regard. Previously family life had been representative of monotony and the antithesis of personal freedom. Now he was starting to see things differently, through different eyes.

Coming to New York had had the unintended consequence of giving him the space to reflect upon and analyse things as never before. And viewed from afar, what had struck him most was the extent to which he was deeply unhappy and unfulfilled. It was this unhappiness, he concluded, that had been responsible for him latching onto Tania and following her to New York in a desperate, even ridiculous, attempt to find her. She represented an escape from the banality of the gym, shopping and sleeping around. It was an oppressive lifestyle, one that involved maintaining an illusion, a persona, designed to exude confidence, poise and status.

The effort expended in the process was enormous, yet still nothing when compared to the erosion of the soul. Seeking meaning in material things — such as clothes, cars, and appearance — had proved nothing if not futile and perverse. Happiness, Brian realised, was the product of personal relationships, the fruits of a life lived for something greater than self. Fear of commitment had crippled him these past two years, and like any fear it had been a fetter on his progress not only as a man but as a human being. It was time to face this fear — face it and conquer it before it rendered him incapable of finding the happiness and purpose he knew now without any shadow of a doubt would make him complete.

Brian Davison was returning home a much changed man from the one who'd left just over a week ago.

## 22

*The beginning is the promise of the end*

One year on from those five memorable days in New York abd life had changed out of all recognition for Brian, the rest of the guys, and also for Tania.

After being forced to resign as a member of the Scottish Parliament, Gareth spent a couple of months trying to work out what to do next. The answer came to him quite unexpectedly one evening when he found himself at a comedy club on Queen Street with a woman he was dating and who brought him along to watch one of her friends perform. It was the first time Gareth had ever been to a comedy club, and he left three hours later determined to pursue a career in stand-up.

A year on and he's plying his new trade at comedy clubs the length and breadth of Scotland. It has to be said, though, he isn't very funny.

Gerry Scott was convicted of shoplifting when his case came up a few months after his arrest in London and his punishment was a ridiculously small fine. However with a criminal record to his name, finding alternative gainful not to mention lucrative employment to support his lifestyle he knew would now be a near impossible task. With this in mind, he decided to use what capital he had left to go into the drugs business with James Traynor. The upshot was tsix years prison sentence after Traynor set him up to take the rap when he got wind that the police were about to move in.

As for Heather, she disappeared as soon as Gerry broke the news that he'd left the legal profession. She then started dating his former partner, Frank Gaffney, who took over the firm. As for Gareth, Heather stopped meeting him for the odd shag as soon as he entered comedy, which to a woman of Heather's ilk was about as much of a turn on as a bowl of boiled shite

Callum's cosy arrangement with his new bank manager was destined not to last. At their second meeting six months after the first, he was curtly informed that his various loans were being called in and that his monthly overdraft was now deemed too high and was being reduced by a whopping fifty percent.

After mulling things over, Callum came to the conclusion that life without being able to shop at Harvey Nichols, drink champagne, drive a top of the range car, and partake the various other luxuries that for him had become necessities, just wasn't worth the candle.

Therefore on a calm, clear day he drove all the way out to the Forth Road Bridge and parked his car at the petrol station adjacent. He then made his way over the bridge on foot with a bottle of his favourite Lansun champagne.

Halfway across he stopped, opened the champagne and drank it from the bottle while reflecting on things. When he was ready, and suitably inebriated, he climbed up on top of the barrier, said his final farewell to the world, and jumped.

Tania ran into an old flame from college at a reunion dance. His name was Gary, he was newly single after emerging from a fifteen year marriage, and from that night on they were inseparable.

Adding to her happiness was the news, three months later, that she was pregnant with twins, thus proving all the doctors who had told her she would never be able to have children completely wrong. They were married soon thereafter and moved to upstate New York, where Gary runs his own accountancy firm. Now and then thoughts of Brian and those glorious few weeks they spent together in Edinburgh enter her head, and whenever they do she wonders if he's as happy as she is.

Speaking of which, Brian knew exactly what he wanted by the time he arrived home from New York. He and Gail had never really stopped loving one another. Deep down they both always felt that their separation was somehow temporary — that in time they'd get back together again. What she had with Graham, Gail knew, could never fill the space vacated by Brian.

This is why when Brian asked her out to dinner as soon as he returned from his trip to New York to talk things over, she said yes.

Over dinner they talked and talked and talked, opening up in the way that only two people who have absolute trust in one other can; Brian admitting to Gail that it was in New York that he realised that what he really wanted out of life was back in Edinburgh, and that after finding the courage to admit it to himself it was like a ton weight being lifted from his shoulders.

She in turn revealed that this is what she'd been waiting to hear for a long time, having known all along that she was still in love with him.

Soon thereafter they were holding hands across the table and making plans. Gail, the next day, called Graham and told him that she was sorry but she was still in love with Brian and that they were going resume their relationshop. Graham responded by calling her a disloyal cunt, before hanging up.

A year on and Brian and Gail have never been happier. As for the single life, you couldn't pay Brian to go back to that — not now, not ever. Waking up next to the same woman every morning, having his kids constantly by his side, this is real happiness. As for Tania, whenever she pops into his head a smile appears, as he finds himself wondering if she ever really existed at all.

End.

Printed in Great Britain
by Amazon